ROCKY MOUNTAIN HIGH

Dan Thomasson and Jack Lang

authorHOUSE®

AuthorHouse™
1663 Liberty Drive
Bloomington, IN 47403
www.authorhouse.com
Phone: 1-800-839-8640

First published by AuthorHouse   05/12/2011

ISBN: 978-1-4567-5684-0 (sc)
ISBN: 978-1-4567-5683-3 (hc)
ISBN: 978-1-4567-5682-6 (e)

Library of Congress Control Number: 2011904360

Printed in the United States of America

Prologue
NEW YEAR'S EVE

He is rolling toward Limon, big motor purring, voices on the radio whanging country songs as bleak as the night. A glance at the dash shows outside temperature at fifteen above zero, a ten-degree dip since he'd left Colorado Springs not a half hour before. The heater is fanning hot air in his face and making him drowsy. He'd given the woman a hot shot and decided at the last minute to take a taste of it that's proving a mistake. He cracks the window and the night's icy dry air jolts him wide awake.

She, curled up in the corner of the passenger side, groans softly but shows no sign of waking. Her face is puffed from his beating. She has clutched her coat in an effort to ward off the cold. Underneath she wears only a thin party dress. One pump had stayed on her foot when he pushed her into the front seat of her Dodge Viper, but she won't need the other. He reminds himself to look for it when he gets back to his condo, and promptly forgets about it.

Eleven-ten at night the road is empty but he keeps his speed at seventy miles an hour, just five over the limit. He isn't much worried about being pulled over so far from the barrooms drawing deputies' attention on the drunkest night of the year, but the risk will rise around Peyton or Calhan or one of the smaller towns along Highway 24. He shouldn't be here, it should have been taken care of by somebody else. But Jack, his newest associate and first choice for this sort of job, can't be found, leaving him to mop up a mess that could send him to the pen at Canon City.

He turns to inform the woman, who makes no reply but who'd likely agree now if her head were clear, "You're one stupid bitch!" When she'd walked in his door tonight she was still pretty, with all the fine soft parts and fun in the sack. She's 34, but it will have to be her last year of prime. This is necessitated by an important business principle in his line of work, which holds that any snitch is owed an abrupt lifespan adjustment.

The wind is churning dust on the plains and eastering clouds turn the night sky even darker. He keeps the radio on low, listening to forecasts that punctuate a stream of country on the Springs' station. Snow is forecast but a disc jockey promises it won't be more than a dusting. He wants this done before getting socked in by weather or leaving tire tracks that might be traced.

It begins to snow in small dry flakes just as he passes Matheson, where the Big Sandy parallels the highway and then heads north before making a sharp bend through the town of Limon fifteen miles onward. He knows of a dirt road that trails south and peters out into the plains. He'd made a drop there before and knows the only resident locals are coyotes and prey critters and maybe sometimes a stargazer, but there's no chance of people out this night.

Slowing, he looks for a small sign warning of an animal crossing. It's just beyond the only tree for miles. He pulls his head closer to the windshield and finds the narrow entrance just as he passes it, backs up and turns onto a path with wheel tracks and a high center. A half-mile along the path dips and disappears in underbrush. He stops well back of the dip, making sure of room to turn around, and cuts the lights, He turns to the girl and says almost affectionately, "Well, Puss, you've run out of road. And nobody feels worse than me about this, except you."

He gets out in his shirtsleeves, adrenalin and dope keeping him from feeling the cold. He opens her door and pats her face to rouse her, pulling her legs outside the car. "Whuh?" she says. "Upsy daisy," he says, left hand under her right arm, hauling her to her feet. "Watch your step now." As she peers down he draws the little .22 from his pocket, puts it to the back of her head and fires once.

She crumples and rolls onto her back, arms flying up across her face in a defensive gesture. She is kicking out frantically and using her elbows to crab-crawl backwards. When he points the gun at her face her arms rise again to ward off the shots. He keeps firing until the gun is empty. Amazing to him, she is still breathing and trying to wriggle away when the gun is empty. *Fuckfuckfuck.* He pulls his switchblade, straddling her, grabbing her by the hair and jabbing the point deep in her back, which is bare of the robe now she's rolled onto elbows and knees. Bubbles of bright red well up when he pulls out the blade with a sucking sound. She moans maybe a minute before slowly going still.

Stepping back, he's amazed by what it took to shut down one small woman. He'd known men stopped as they stood, first shot bouncing around in the skull and stirring brains to soup, but this hard-headed bitch took death for a dance. It might have made him proud of her if he'd been the slightest sentimental. Now he drags her farther out into the prairie and goes back to the car for his road-trip groceries, pulls out a jar of peanut butter and unloosens the lid as he returns to her body. Dipping his fingers in the peanut butter, he smears it over her hands and feet and head, mixing it with her blood.

"When those coyotes get a whiff of Peter Pan and come to the picnic, you can kiss your ass and pretty face goodbye," he says. He jogs back to the Viper and feels a light sweat on his forehead as he keys the horsepower. Bouncing off down the track, the bottom scraping, he cranks the volume on the radio in time to hear a nasal wail, *"How can I miss you if you won't go awayyy . . ."*

Behind him the frail form twitches, whimpers, goes still, stirs again. After a little while she begins to move, something between a crawl and a wriggle, toward she doesn't know where, through the coldest night so far this winter.

1

What Sam Tanner did on his workdays was often a dangerous adventure. He'd admit it, except to his elderly parents, his young daughters, any of the neighbors. Not that he cared about giving offense, he just didn't want them knowing what he was deeply into, the guns and drugs and cycle thugs. His last assignment involved infiltrating a white supremacist group in the Midwest and now he was messing with something about as deadly, federal forms.

Two months back some routine paperwork that landed on his desk took him into a gun-drawn showdown with two crack-dealing members of the Crips gang out of Los Angeles. This afternoon he expected to buy some guns from their organization, if they didn't do something stupid. In which case things could get considerably uglier. He'd much prefer it if they would simply take the money, hand over the weapons and lead the way to their employer, who might be persuaded to divulge some commercial secrets. Of course government regulation is seldom appreciated and, as he often said to his wife, a public servant sometimes has to make hard choices. The two Crips in question had not shown great business sense to this point and their supervisor, whose acquaintance Tanner sought, could be disagreeable.

"Who tops your do-list today?" Sally asked him that morning, day six of a diet that gave him a dab of yogurt and granola for breakfast and a hunger that left him edgy all day.

He looked around to see if the girls were in earshot and lowered his voice, "Buff".

"Why do you call him that?"

Tanner drained the last of his coffee. "He's big and he's ugly and he's a fat fucker.......ergo Buff."

"Makes perfect sense then," Sally said.

"It's what I do, make perfect sense of things. Probably why I was needed here in the Colorado Springs office."

"A man who makes perfect sense of things is needed in every office."

"Yeah but," Tanner said, "right here is where we got this great abundance of low lifes."

"Who'd have thought it, here amid the purple mountains' majesty?" Sally was being typically caustic and couldn't help adding, "Not to mention the fruited plains."

"Practically nobody," Sam agreed."

Tanner had transferred to the Colorado Springs office of ATF understanding that the surrounding military bases made it a hotbed for illegal weapons and drug trading. Soon enough he was thinking maybe the mountain outpost should be the agency's regional headquarters and Denver the satellite office. He'd avidly read everything he could about the town because, though raised in northern Virginia, he'd actually been born and spent the first two years of his life right in the Springs. His father had been a flack for the FBI who'd gotten sent here for some offense he didn't discuss, brushing it off as carbon paper wastage or something about smudges on his white shirts, two Bureau obsessions in the day. That was the Sixties when this was a payback posting for that agency, but these days, for Sam's own outfit, here was a plum.

Colorado Springs, overlooked by Pikes Peak and the dramatic rise of the southern Rockies' eastern front, was home to some 400,000 mostly respectable civilian souls leading lives of order and prosperity in one of nature's wonderlands. It was also the location of the army's Fort Carson, Peterson Air Force Base, the Air Force Academy and the United States Olympic Training Center, as well as headquarters for a passel of right-leaning broadcast evangelists who gave politicians in Washington heartburn. Tanner quickly comprehended that Colorado Springs had more avowed Christians front and center, more healthy hard bodies swarming the mountains and more horny soldiers everywhere than anybody can shake a stick at.

The frequent deployment of brigades of the 4th Infantry Division for a year at a time to hot sandy places where there's no place fun to spend their pay meant the troops came home with cash to blow, as soldiers have done since the invention of forward march. Gathering around to welcome home the heroes was a patriotic multitude of tattoo artists, gun dealers, drug dealers, strippers, pimps, whores, loan sharks, repo men, process servers and bail bondsmen, who in turn attracted cops of all varieties.

Colorado Springs, looking a picture book place to raise kids, was also the distribution center of a methamphetamine industry that stretched from Canada to Mexico and the Great Plains to California, as well as a hub of illegal weapons trade.

Tanner didn't understand much of this then. He didn't know the how of it or any of the who. He was just the new guy with suspicions and ambition.

"There's lots here to do for a man of enterprise and genius," Tanner assured his wife.

Claire and Haley came clumping down the stairs and ran to Tanner for hugs, smelling of toothpaste, shampoo, laundered dresses and little girl. He pretended to chomp their necks, one after the other, setting off giggles.

"Okay, girls, I've gotta go get the bad guys," he told them.

"Why, Daddy?" asked Haley with a six-year-old's calculation, knowing the answer and grinning.

"To keep you safe." It got him another hug.

Claire, the fastest ten-year-old striker in Pinion Hills girls soccer, had some issues lately with her dad. "You coming to my practice?" She already knew the answer to that one, too, and didn't like it. He hadn't made it to one this fall.

"Not this time, sugar. Your Saturday game though, I'll make it or try dying." The wordplay nearly got him a smile but Claire settled on a stink-eye.

"You'll be home for dinner?" Sally asked.

"Expect so. What we having?"

"Roast pork and *papas a la huancaina*."

"That what I think it is?"

"It means potatoes with cheese sauce, man of genius."

"I was going to say that."

"Six o'clock?"

"About." He gave her the look. "I'll come back.

"I know."

No matter what, he'd always told her, I will come back. She'd promised him, I'll believe you will. Sometimes they said it when they parted and, sometimes, in their bed before they slept and after what they'd done that made them sleepy. The pledge meant more to them than it would to most couples. Every morning he left the house there was a chance he wouldn't come back except of course they believed he would. He'd said so, and when he said he'd do something, Sam did it.

Sally was mainly a mom and had been for 10 years now, but until they married she had been a NOC, or non-official cover agent of the CIA, which meant she too had worked undercover. When they met he was working in security for the State Department, providing protection for diplomats and embassies in South America. But neither could see how a marriage would last with one or both on distant assignments for weeks at a time.

Tanner quit diplomatic security and transferred to ATF, where adrenalin would remain his daily friend but he wouldn't normally be away more than a few nights at a time. Sally resigned from the CIA and became a homemaker, if one with different skills from those in her neighborhood of Colorado Springs. Sure, she could make apple pie about as good as any American mom or even whip up *papas a la huancaina*, but she could also crack a sternum. Someday soon her daughter's Claire's soccer coach could learn for himself how fingers came unhinged, if he got around to putting a hand on Sally where he kept putting his eyes. Most important to the Tanners' marriage, Sally would do the waiting without complaining about it. She'd been *there* herself and she knew what Sam could do. It came down to belief in the church of two, he'd come home *no matter what.*

The gunfight that broke out in the center of Colorado Springs that afternoon between the feds and the Crips was an unforeseen event that had its origins in someone having to fill out a government form. There were to be so many more consequences and homicides in coming months that those in Tanner's chain of command would have plenty of time afterward to reflect on how it all began with single sheet of paper.

To legally get a gun anywhere in the U.S., a buyer has to complete Transaction Record 4473 requiring a verifiable name and address and the answers to a list of questions so ponderously obvious it seems silly to ask them. "Are you under indictment in any court for a felony?" and "Have you ever been adjudicated mentally defective?" Answer yes to either one, no gun. Another goes, "Are you a fugitive from justice?" Say yes and again no gun for you, but you do get an ATF agent with his own gun coming to take you into custody. So who'd say yes? Thousands of Americans every year. An apparent reason is the bold type at the bottom of the page that promises a false answer to any question is a crime punishable as a felony. So knuckleheads admit to being felons so as not to be charged as felons – without stopping to think, *oh never mind,* and quit filling out the form. But as a circuit judge once told Tanner, "Hardly a one of the characters who'll come before my court this morning has the foresight of lunchtime."

One way to scam the system is to send a straw purchaser with a clean record to the dealer. There is, though, a trick aspect to the paperwork – called collation. Anytime two or more guns are bought from a licensed dealer within a five-day period by any persons residing at the same address, their separate forms are compared. ATF is alerted. An agent is on the way.

So it was that back that spring, Tanner's third day in the Colorado

Springs office, his assignment had been to check out the purchase of a Star .38 revolver on a Monday by a Jamal Jones and a Tec-9, 9mm handgun on the next Thursday by a Jerome Kinney, who both listed their addresses as Apt. 3-D, Rockledge Gardens.

As Tanner pulled up to the yellow brick complex he saw, standing to either side of the iron-grilled entrance, two young black men in gangsta pants and blue bandannas snugged to their heads. One held a plastic carry case for a Tec-9 semi-automatic pistol and neither looked pleased to see him. *Not Mormon missionaries then*, Tanner suggested to himself.

They were edging away as he got out of the car.

"Good morning sirs, fine day for felony," he called out as he approached, "Have you seen my cat? Blue? Cross-eyed? Pulling a wagon?"

Talking weirdly but almost making sense sometimes worked and put a suspect off balance, let Tanner get close enough to where his size and presence could dominate. The thing was to keep coming and talking. "Her name's Fred. Probably queer. Episcopalian for sure. There's a large reward." His patter had them hesitating until he got to twenty feet.

"ATF. Show me your ID."

They started to go for their guns. He got to his first.

"Don't do it," he said, Glock steady in his fist, their hands hovering at their belts. "You don't want to do it."

They didn't want to do it. Watching the Glock, they started backing up.

"Get your hands away from your guns. Show me IDs," he ordered.

They broke and ran into the building. Tanner chased after with no hopes of running them down. His time on VMI's defensive line was a dozen years behind him and he couldn't have caught whippets like these even then. But he followed where he knew they were likely headed, up three flights and down a hall where they ducked into a doorway and slammed it shut. He looked at the locked door, listened to their mutterings inside, sighed. He stomped back down stairs, went to his car, popped the trunk, grabbed his armored vest and shotgun and a fistful of shells. He could see faces peeking down at him through their third-floor window. He racked the shotgun and pointed it at the window as he walked back to the building.

A bald man with a Dachshund on a leash was coming out of a door when Tanner reached the second floor. Tanner turned him around. "Go back inside, stay there, call 911, tell them officer needs assistance."

On the third-floor Tanner again pounded the door.

"Yoooo-hoo. Open up, boys. I'm here for you," he sang out. No one responded but it sounded like several men moving around inside.

He waited there for backup, hearing the sirens coming, and while he did the three Crips in the apartment dropped one by one from their third-floor balcony onto the parking lot below. Arnold Silvers, 56, in 2-D, the bald man with the dachshund, said later he was looking out his window and watched them take the thirty-foot drop. Two skinny ones took off like bats from hell, he said, but the big heavy one fell and hobbled to a metallic green Cadillac that sped him away.

Tanner and four CSPC officers were standing by 3-D's door, backs to the wall, readying to bust down the door, when they heard footsteps on the stairwell behind them and female voice said, "Hey, that's our apartment. What's going on?"

Tanysha Hynson, nineteen and very pretty, and Brenda Brown, twenty and not so much, came home to learn they'd made some unwise choices this social season. After some consideration of alternatives, none happy, the girls gave their permission to search, which turned up two AR-15s, a 12-gauge pump, two Tec-9s, a Taurus .45, four Sig .40s and 500 rounds of ammunition, plus a number of plastic bags with cocaine residue and a case of baking soda.

"Kiss and tell," Tanner urged, "can be a good thing."

Miss Hynson and Miss Brown, shown the evidence found inside their own apartment, took that advice after some further discussion. They gave up detailed descriptions, the street names and hangouts of four Crips who'd been crashing at their pad off and on since they'd met the younger two at Club Divine back in May.

It was the weapons cache that would keep ATF in pursuit of their swift asses. The drugs were ordinarily DEA's worry but the surest way to track them. A seller of crack will be as discreet as he can but in the retail end he's got to be where the customer can find him. An informant with the taste located Jamal and Jerome, known on the street as Stinks and Boo, working a corner on East Bijou for an enormous crew chief with the street name of Cricket but known to the watching ATF agents as Buff - Big Ugly Fat Fucker.

A man who said his name was Gomer approached the Crips' corner outlet one day and bought a hundred dollars worth. He returned a few days later and said he could take a half ounce. The next week he was back talking of how he had a territory down the road in Limon and somebody was muscling him, and he was looking for a nine millimeter and some Tec-9s.

"We'll talk to somebody," Cricket said. Come back in an hour."

Gomer did. Cricket said he could put his hands on the pistol, one Intertec and a Mac-10 and set the price at two thousand dollars. Gomer said he'd get the money by the next day. They agreed on 3 p.m. at the parking lot of Continental Music Store on east Platte Avenue.

The man called Gomer went back to his office in the federal building to do the deskwork for setting up the buy. He couldn't use government funds to buy illegal weapons without signing for the advance, and he had to set up surveillance and backup. That was going to take all the manpower available to ATF – in this town, on that day, just three men.

2

Tanner sat behind the wheel of a dirty Crown Vic in the parking lot of Fargo Pizza with an open view of the north and west sides of the music store. The sides of the building he couldn't see were under surveillance by DEA agents in two other cars. Fifteen minutes passed before Tanner and his partner Ben Hayden saw undercover agent Charles Gadsen drive up in a blue van and park by the store's rear entrance.

Gadsen, known to the Crips as Gomer, got out of the van and put a cell phone to his ear. The wire he wore transmitted his words clearly, "I'm here, where're you? . . . Right, see you now."

Tanner watched as a green Cadillac with gold top and blackened windows pulled into the lot and sat there a minute before two men got out and entered Gadsen's van.

"You want to buy crack?" came a voice on the wire.

"Naw, man (Gadsen's voice, indignant) I'm here for a nine and a Tec."

"Let's go then."

Gadsen's van rolled off the lot onto Tijuana Street and a maroon Buick Regal with two other men inside sped through the lot and began following it. Tanner began trailing the vehicles on parallel streets, going right on De Cortez when they went right on Dale, then speeding ahead so he could intercept. He didn't like the direction the pursuit was going. The van had left the business district and driven into an older residential neighborhood of nice homes, where he could see people in their yards enjoying the sun of a warm afternoon.

As the cars approached the intersection with Querida Drive, static made conversation unintelligible, with only occasional phrases coming through clearly. Tanner could make out "motherfucker" and "nigga" and "bitch" punctuating every sentence, but the tone indicated everything was okay until Gadsen's voice suddenly became high-pitched and loud. "What is this? What you doing?"

Everybody listening knew what. Tanner stomped the gas and turned right on Querida, where he saw the van pulled to the curb and Gadsen standing at its right rear facing two Crips and two more gang members coming toward him from the Buick Regal, which had cut them off.

Tanner and Hayden piled out just as Gadsen shouted "Police," a futile effort to stop the guns coming out. Gadsen cleared his gun just as the closest Crip drew his own out of a long dark coat, a Mac-10.

When the gunfire started Tanner had so much adrenaline pumping in his system that he experienced it in slow motion. Drawing his gun, he held fire as everybody else's weapons went off because he could see two children downrange riding Big Wheels on the sidewalk. Then the fat Crip ran to the Buick and hopped behind the wheel and Tanner got his sights on the back of his head, firing as the car hit a road bump and the rear bounced up, bullets thunking into the trunk. Now the green Cadillac came backing down the street toward the gunfight and the Crips ran toward it. One Crip fell but got up and ran to the Caddy clutching his side, hopping in as it sped away.

The gunfight actually lasted only half a minute, though to Tanner in the moment it seemed to go on and on. In his ears it had sounded as if something distant, and muted, like popping corn. On the recording from the tape machine worn under Gadsen's left armpit and played later in court, it was shockingly loud and sounded like twenty-five shots in two exchanges separated by the loud panting of Gadsen as he pursued the Crips up the street.

It was as if the gunfire blew the static out of the wire. A voice at the end was perfectly clear – "I'm shot, I'm shot, I'm shot. Goddamn. Oh shit. Oh shit."

Sally was putting dishes in the washer and the girls were upstairs doing homework when the doorbell dinged. Opening it she found Lena McTier, a neighbor from down the block and wife of a CSPD officer.

Lena was a plain, blunt woman. "Sally, I'm here with real bad news. Sam has been shot."

"Not Sam," said Sally.

"Yes, Sally, he has. Let's sit down."

"No, he's not."

"Yes, it came over the net an ATF agent was shot and Jerry suited up and went in. Some of the guys who were off today and know Sam did, too. They're out looking for the shooter."

"Wasn't Sam."

Sally walked back into the kitchen. Lena followed and didn't know what to say next. The woman was in complete denial.

"Um, maybe you should call his office, Sal."

"I don't need to, wasn't him."

The phone rang.

"Hello. Oh hi, Hon, we were just talking about you."

"Afraid I'm going to be held up here awhile," Sam told her.

"Um-hmm, something to do with a shooting?"

"Wasn't me."

"Didn't believe it even a minute. Who was it, how bad?"

"Gadsen. Not clear yet but signs are okay. Bullet in the lower leg, another in his side. They're working on him now. It was almost a lot worse. Crip pulls a Mac-10 on Gadsen from six feet away, close enough to saw him in half, and it doesn't fire. Tell you something else, I'm not a fan anymore of the nine millimeter. Gadsen fires right into the guy and the fat fuck doesn't go down, just backs away, makes it to a car and hauls ass. I could'a put a round or two in him myself."

"You'll get him though. Look for a guy with extra holes."

"Why didn't I think of that?" said Sam.

"You can't think of everything. Want me to hold your dinner?"

"No, I'm going to be here late."

"Got your two favorite food groups, meat and potatoes."

"No. I'll just grab something here. Don't wait up."

Sally put down the phone and looked at Lena. "Told you so."

Lena stared at her in wonder, shaking her head.

"It's like this," Sally said. "We've got kind of an understanding. I'd just know."

While the trauma docs tended Gadsden, Tanner sat in the reception area and called his supervisor Josh Groton who was in Denver for the day. It took a few rings before the boss answered in a muffled voice. "Is this an emergency? We've got the team from Washington in here."

"The buy went bad and Charles is down with two bullets," Tanner replied. "I think he's going to be okay."

"Jesus Christ. What went wrong? Never mind, I'm on my way. Where are you?

"Colorado Springs General. I think we wounded two of these guys and Hayden went in pursuit while I had to get Gadsen to the hospital. They got away from Hayden but the CPSD has an all points out for them. At least one of 'em, maybe two, has got to get medical help. We'll find them. "

"Be there in an hour, bringing some help," Groton said and hung up.

A commotion behind Tanner spun his attention to a stumpy man with an almost orange complexion bellowing about "the maniac who was driving that car." It was Chief Bertram Beetle of the CSPD, shaking his finger and shouting at two of his officers. One patrolman mumbled something and pointed toward Tanner, who took a deep breath. There was little regard and no affection at all between this chief and any federal agency. Beetle had been smarting all year under bad publicity about his department's failure to stem the illegal traffic in military hardware, which was the reason for ATF's newly established office here.

Walking over to the group, Tanner said as politely as he could, "May I help you, chief?"

"What the hell do you think you were doing driving my streets that way?" the chief demanded.

"Trying to save my partner's life. Would that be a good reason? If you have any complaints about that, take them up with my boss."

The chief clomped off and his two officers looked back, one fighting a smile and the other giving Tanner a quick wink.

At 9 p.m. just after Groton arrived, a surgeon emerged from the ER and told them Gadsen was going to be fine. They could go in to see him if they kept it short.

The agent was propped up, his eyes open but dozey when they opened the curtain around his bed.

"I won't ask how you feel, pardner," Groton said.

"I'd have to say shitty if you did, sir."

"You up to a short explanation of what happened?"

"Sure. The son of a bitch was going to rip us off. Keep the guns and also the money. If he hadn't fumbled with the Mac 10, I would be dead. I think it jammed. I had time to give the signal and Sam and Hayden made it before the first shot was fired."

"Good enough," said Groton. "Get some rest. The same goes for you Sam. Oh, yeah. Don't worry about the police chief. I'll take care of that bastard and if he wants to complain to Washington, he can. I can't think he will, after all we've been doing his job for him. You'll both have to answer to a shooting incident team but this one's righteous."

3

Late on a clear night in a cluttered house on a one-block street at the edge of Fort Carson, the phone rings and a naked man gets up from his couch to answer it. "Yeah?" He listens and says, "Yeah, I'll do it. But it's fucking two in the morning and I'm half wasted. Don't make a lot'a sense to be driving around this time of night when a cop'll check out anything that moves. Okay, your call. By four," and hangs up.

The girl on the couch is naked, too. She has a line of coke on the glass top coffee table and is about to snort it through a rolled-up bill.

"Uh-uh," he says, licking a finger, rolling it in the powder and rubbing it on his gums. "Mine." He reaches over and gives her breast a painful squeeze. "Get the hell out, I got business."

It's a stupid assignment but he's been crossways with the Pachecos and can't be that again. He's too deep in his own angry thoughts to even look up when she stalks out of the den swinging her bare ass and not looking back, her fuck-you fingers standing at attention, and locks herself in the bathroom.

This is crazy, he tells himself. Why'n hell do they want goodies at an hour when any car on the road looks hinky? He should have a say on delivery times. He goes to his bedroom and slips on a hoodie and cargo pants. He pulls a cardboard box from under his bed, lifts out a roll of cash that he slips in a pocket and a kilo of coke and a baggie of meth he packs in a yellow plastic Homer Simpson book bag. From a closet he pulls out a heavy green duffle stuffed with weapons. Lugging it to his garage, he drops the drugs on the seat of his F-150 Pickup and the weapons on the floor of the passenger side. He sits behind the wheel letting the cab and engine warm, figuring it will take about an hour down I-25 to the Trinidad turnoff, another twenty minutes on the gravel road before the rendezvous, and he could be home before sunup. Better take it easy all the way, he tells himself, but he doesn't. He's off with a squeal of tires, forgetting to turn on his headlights. He hasn't remembered his wallet, either.

Rookie Officer Jay Friedlander isn't halfway through his midnight to eight when he looks up from his roadie of coffee to see the truck cheat a stop. Then he notices no lights. He hits his siren and flashers, and the jerk accelerates away. Friedlander radios his position to dispatch and asks for the other officer on night patrol to block off access to I-25. In seconds his squad car is on the big pickup's tail and swinging around to force it onto the shoulder.

The truck clips a phone pole, spins half around and stalls out on the front lawn of a house. His interceptor cutting off the only access to the street, Friedlander is on it like a bird on a bug, hopping from the car, his pistol aimed at the driver's head as he shouts, "Show both hands out the window." He brings his cuffs down hard on the driver's wrists, opens the door and pulls him out, forcing him face down on the ground. By the book, he thinks. The man mumbles something into the earth and Friedlander leans closer to hear his lament.

"Why the fuck?" the man's complaining. "Why. Fucking. Me."

The man is speaking to the cosmos but it's the cop who answers. "Well, it ain't for the fucking Safe Driver Award."

Sam Tanner pulled his plain wrapper sedan into the parking garage and stopped in one of the spaces marked "Reserved for Abe Goldfarb and Associates." He thought it probably one of the lamer efforts to mislead a poorly informed citizenry, but everybody working for the Bureau of Alcohol, Tobacco, Firearms and Explosives had to be careful in the still-wild West where guns outnumbered people. Before getting out of the car he opened the console, took out his Glock and slid it into the holster on his belt. With that, and his locked and loaded briefcase, he considered himself fully armed for bureaucracy, always a tricky adversary on the first day back from two weeks' leave.

He'd been at his desk ten minutes when Groton the Resident Agent in Charge knocked on his door, offering a cup of coffee and plopping his wide rear in a narrow chair. "Having fun?" asked the boss.

"Getting a government-issued hard-on here going over my per diem."

"Whoa, you owe the cuss bucket." The office had agreed to a system of fines to cut down on swearing. Every oath cost a buck to go toward the Christmas party.

"There's no penalty for filthy talk if you're refined and don't actually use bad words. And I didn't use a goddam one."

"It's just one shitty dollar, pay up." Both walked over to the can labeled Only You Can Prevent Smut and fed it their pocket shrapnel.

Tanner considered Groton the best boss he'd had and a good friend to have in a bad place. Groton was a former Georgia state trooper who'd been shot twice in the line of duty, once surviving a gunfight on a bus.

"All you got to know about your ordinary bus battle," Groton had counseled him, "is you can't run and you can't hide, and so you really cannot miss your shots. Or you'll be terminally disappointed in yourself."

Today Groton had good news for the staff about some shots not missed, and the happy consequences of putting nine millimeter perforations in a couple of Crips. He looked around the conference room smiling widely and said, "A certain Keshawn Wheeler, aka Cricket and previously known to some of you here as the Big Ugly Fat Fucker, has rolled over on some miscreants in Colorado Springs that require our attention. I think we're going to be busy here awhile." He began summarizing a report from the LA office on the Crip who had turned up at a hospital there with assorted bullet holes that he claimed had occurred when he was robbed by persons unknown in Watts.

That story might have held up except for the fact one Jamal Jones had previously been found unconscious on a sidewalk in south Colorado Springs with a bullet in his abdomen and, when patched and revived, had given up Keshawn Wheeler as his crew chief and partner in what the bureau was calling The Gunfight at Oh Shit and Querida. It took little time for the ATF to follow Jones' leads and track down Wheeler asleep on his gurney in LA and lock him to it.

"It's a wonder he survived the trip all the way home to LA before going to a hospital for treatment," Groton said, "I'm guessing all that bulk protected his vitals some, but it also collected our slugs. Good shooting Sam, and you, too, Charley." He nodded at Agent Charles Gadsen, sitting with his bandaged leg elevated. "That's now two for you."

Ballistics had shown the bullet that passed through Jamal Jones and lodged in his belt came from Gadsen's pistol. The tests on a bullet taken out of Wheeler also matched up with Gadsen's weapon. Two others slugs pried out of Wheeler's mighty posterior came from the weapons of Tanner and Agent Ben Hayden. Forensics had tightly tied both Crips to a shootout with three federal officers.

"Folks'll be scratching heads over this one for years," Groton said. "Guy is shot by three different guns at one time and doesn't drop. He escapes the scene. He makes it a thousand miles across the country and he lives. And we got incredibly lucky, too. The odds against us getting that many good readable slugs from one shooting incident are higher than Pikes Peak."

With ballistics tying them to the gunfight with the agents, each of the Crips faced reams of local and federal charges, which was turning them into an a cappella chorus. "Too bad that you couldn't be there to hear 'em sing," Groton told Gadsen, who was still on medical leave and had dropped in the office to pick up mail and gossip. "They're giving up each other, their mamas and baby sisters and their pit bulls. But what's important for this office, they're giving up a local family. Some people called Pachecos."

As Groton explained it, the Crips were buying cocaine at $300 an ounce in Los Angeles and bringing it to Colorado Springs where they cooked it up with baking soda in a microwave and turned it into rock selling for $1100 per ounce. They controlled a substantial part of the crack market in the Springs. According to Jones and Wheeler, they'd bought most of their weaponry from an outfit they believed had control of methamphetamine distribution through much of the Rockies and the plains. The Crips didn't deal in meth locally and this local gang weren't into coke and crack, so they didn't war.

"Wheeler tells us the Colorado Springs bunch are boasting they can get you whatever you want, automatic rifles, silencers, anything that goes bang." Groton said. "And he'll so testify about his dealings with one of them. It's a guy named Richard Tirado, who it so happens recently fucked up and I've been informed is currently in custody. The Crips have given us another name that we haven't come across anywhere else, said to be Tirado's honcho, guy called Ramon."

Tanner got the assignment to follow up on Tirado through Chuck Dennison at the El Paso County Parole Office, who'd called ATF and left a voice message as soon as the arrest report hit his desk. When Tanner called him, Dennison picked up on the second ring, choking. "Sorry. Swallowed my donut wrong. Listen, how 'bout dropping over? I want to make your day."

Dennison's office was plainly the space of someone overworked and under-rewarded: small and cluttered with stacks of folders on every surface. Even his phone topped a pile of reports.

"Take the perp seat," he said, waiving him to a wooden upright chair in front of his desk. "Have to say, you don't look the worse for wear, getting shot at and missed and then shouted at by Chief Beetle, otherwise known in the halls of justice as Dung."

Tanner shrugged. "He does have a way of latching onto a bit of dung and rolling it up into something big and useless. But I know he'll come to see my finer points. It's just he doesn't seem to believe me when I look him in the eye and say 'I'm from the federal government and I'm here to help you.'"

Dennison grinned. "You say that to him?"

"Every time we meet. Which reminds me, 'I'm from the federal government and . . .'"

"Actually, the way it goes this morning is, I'm from county law enforcement and I'm here to help you suits from Washington. I'm drawing your attention to a citizen who could best serve his country in a secure government facility. And I'm thinking you might want him to sing for his federal suppers."

Dennison explained that Richard Tirado, aka Tick-Tock, b. Bakersville, Ca., 5-10-73, with a measured IQ of 141 according to one psychological assessment, was a social disappointment. Tirado had spent most of his childhood in and out of foster homes after his mother and father were incarcerated for drug violations, and since age eighteen had diligently built a record of narcotics, theft, assault and firearms offenses.

Tirado had broken parole a year ago, skipping from his address of record after missing his last mandatory meeting with the parole officer. Dennison had looked for him with no luck. Tirado was in the wind.

"But now this, something to make his fourth felony conviction." Dennison handed over a report from the Fountain Police Department dated yesterday. Fountain, the last stop out of Colorado Springs on I-25 before Pueblo, had sprung up in the high desert as a bedroom community for soldiers at Fort Carson, home of the Army's Mountain Warfare School and the famed 10th Mountain Division. It was a town with too-many stoplights and a sufficiency of bars, used car dealerships, drive-ins, big box stores and a long sprawl of modest homes for transient military personnel, their yards spilling plastic playgrounds for kids in primary colors. It also had a small and poorly paid police force, the youngest member of which was a real go-getter, at least on the night before.

The report was straightforward. It stated that at 2:30 a.m., Officer Jay Freidlander had been on patrol in the center of town when he saw a red and white Ford F150 pickup driving erratically with its lights off. When Freidlander tried to stop the car, a short chase took place, ending with the truck in the front yard of a house on Route 83. Tirado, the officer discovered, was wanted on outstanding warrants. His troubles deepened when Friedlander poked through the truck and found a Chinese-made AK47, a sawed-off shotgun, nine handguns, a kilo of cocaine, three ounces of methamphetamine and several U.S. passports. In Tirado's right front pocket Friedlander found a roll of bills that he logged as totaling $9,115.

Tanner whistled. "You say this character's got an IQ of 141?"

"So it says here. But, it would appear that he now is a vendor of condiments that make your brain go brzzt."

"And fond of his produce."

"Apparently."

Tanner slowly hefted his big frame from the small chair. "Looks like I owe you one, Chuck. Think I'll wander south to the Fountain jailhouse and see if Tirado wants to trade his way out of a lasting domestic arrangement with some butt bandits. I've said it before and I'll say it again, law and order is sure to benefit from an informant looking at twenty to life."

A sheriff's deputy led a short, thickly muscled man into the interview room where Tanner had been waiting for ten minutes. Tirado had close-cropped hair and a thin blond mustache. Around his right forearm wrapped a black-ink tattoo of a snake, on the back of his left hand was one of a small red rose.

Tanner indicated the chair across the table. "Please sit, I'm Sam Tanner, ATF."

Tirado was a heftier man than Tanner had expected for a supposed meth user. If he had the habit bad, it had come on him so fast his failing appetite wasn't showing yet.

"They call you 'Tick-Tock?"

Tirado nodded.

"Anything you want?"

"Can I smoke?" Tanner nodded and Tirado's hand shook as he fished a cigarette out of his breast pocket and lip up.

"Anything else?"

"How 'bout I get out of here?"

"I was coming to that." Tanner opened the folder on the table and flipped through a few pages. "There's half a dozen federal charges that apply in your case. With your rap sheet, you'll be on a walker before you see sky beyond the big wall. Or, we can help each other."

Tirado looked hard at Tanner but couldn't hold the stare. He took a last drag and stubbed out the butt.

"You know what I can do for you," Tanner prodded. "Help you get less time, your choice of prison, cell of your own."

"How do I know you'll deliver?"

Tanner stuck out his hand to Tirado, "My word."

Tirado looked at the hand. Slowly, he took it. "You don't want me. You want who I work for. I can give them to you. But how do I stay alive when I'm doing it?"

"You watch your back. You do Pacheco with me and I watch your back, too. I can't promise you'll be bullet proof. It's a sneaky business and you chose your own associates. But I'll tell you this here and now, as long as your information's good, your well-being matters to me.

But, you try jamming me, you'll find yourself without one friend out there."

Tirado pulled out another cigarette and couldn't find a match, looked a question at Tanner who shook his head but raised his eyebrows in a question of his own.

Taking a deep breath, Tirado said, "I can give you a case that'll make your career. How'd you like to bust one of the biggest meth and gun operations in this part of the country?"

Tanner smiled and waited.

"I can make the intros and I can vouch for you."

Tanner knew he'd now get the pitch he'd heard a hundred times from jailed informants: "But I can't do it from here. I have to be out of jail to do it. They took my stash when they busted me."

True. The wad of cash the arresting officer found on Tirado was confiscated as evidence along with the weapons. Tanner also knew that as soon as word of his arrest hit the street it was almost certain his own rat pack would have raided his home and made off with everything they could hide or hock. Tirado was looking like a mid-level player in the meth scene, possibly someone even higher, but whatever his income of a week ago he'd have no collateral now.

To pop him loose, Tanner's Rules would apply. The first one was don't stand bond officially but force him to post his own bail, using money Tanner could provide as an advance for information. That set the hook before he got on the street. Tanner's Rule Number Two was all fuckups fuck up, get caught doing other crimes, overdosing or trying to give the slip. So he'd be at the door of the pokey to go operational and make buys from the minute the informant stepped in the sunshine.

"We can work it out," Tanner told the smaller man who was having trouble keeping eye contact. "I'm going to have to convince myself you just aren't a scammer who'll rabbit the first hour out. That's going to take a few sessions with you giving me information I can check out."

Tanner stood and knocked on the door. When two deputies appeared he said, "We're done for the time being. I'll be back tomorrow."

Before leaving the jail, Tanner stuck his head in Sheriff Jim Conner's office.

"Just wanted to let you know I may have a live one in your hotel and could use your help keeping him under wraps until I'm ready to provide him with the wherewithal to spring himself. Guy's name is Tirado, street name's Tick-Tock, a habitual in on guns, meth and passport problems out of Fountain."

"Believe I heard about this one. Whatever you need," Conner said.

"If you've got room, keep him in solitary. I don't want him talking to anybody or making any calls or being visited by anyone, including a lawyer if possible. If a shyster does show would you please call me right away . . .

"You got it."

Tanner had one more stop, a storefront business on El Paso Street with a sign in the window, "Quick and Easy Bail Bonds." The receptionist wasn't at her desk, so he called out "Sid" and walked a short hall to a back office where he found a bald man almost as broad as his desk munching a mouthful of pastrami and rye.

Sid Glick swallowed, leaking mustard at the corner of his mouth. Wiping it, he rose a few inches from his chair and settled back as if hoisting the whole load exceeded their level of acquaintance and said, "Come in, Agent Tanner, have a seat. Hell, have my office. Have the whole building and my house and my cat. Whatever my government requires of me, be my guest, take it. It's all been mortgaged anyway to pay my taxes for foreign wars, one of which I financed entirely. Of course I understand you're just doing your job."

"You all done?" Tanner asked and sat.

"Well I could go on."

"I have no doubts. But we got business."

Glick wadded the remains of his lunch and tossed it in a trashcan. He rocked back, locking his ham-size hands behind his huge head. Glick did lawmen favors when he could and was known for asking only two things in return: he'd make money on the deal and he got to yank their chains.

His chain well pulled, Tanner could proceed. "I've got something underway and could use a little cooperation. A potentially good informant is up on gun charges and sometime in a couple of weeks, I'm going to ask you to bond him out in my custody. But we want it to seem the money is his. So we'll provide him cash to pay you the ten percent, and he in turn will give it to you. Make it look on paper like it's all his deal."

"Any time frame here?"

"Not sure exactly. I need to verify what he tells me."

"And if he skips?"

"He won't," Tanner said with more confidence than he felt. "I'll be eyeballing him. He also needs our protection. But if he blows the deal, he will be a federal fugitive and I will personally hunt him down. You know you won't get hurt. Uncle's got good collateral."

"I've heard that," said Glick. "Put me down for Yellowstone."

4

"So what do we do about Tirado?"

"Nothing," the woman said. "He got himself caught so he gets himself out. We can't be connected to him."

"What if he rolls? He is up for the long term this time."

Maria Pacheco looked through dusty windows at pedestrians on the corners and peered in her rearview mirror, checking out the cars parked behind on South Platt. It was her habit, consider before reply. Sweat beaded at her temples and she dabbed it with a tissue before turning to study the thin man next to her. Tomas Rahall had the look of a manikin put in the field to discourage crows, his hair in tufts, cheeks dead white and blue eyes empty as a Colorado summer sky. She suspected she knew what Rahall himself would do if he had been arrested.

"If he runs his mouth we will know it quick enough," she said. "The longer he stays inside the better indication that he hasn't ratted, isn't being used." She put a hand to Rahall's shoulder, more gesture than a touch. "You know he is like a son to me, Tomas."

Rahall didn't know anything of the sort, but even if true it had little meaning if this plump, fifty some matron in the polka dot dress felt threatened. Her placid manner deceived, like the Gila monster. Maria Pacheco not only looked like a mother, she was one four times over. Three of her children lived well and respectably in Mexico, and her eldest son Ramon was, at 30, *Capitan* in one of the most lucrative gun and drug operations in the West. Maria had put her son in that position and if he didn't do the job well she'd put him where he'd dearly wish he had. Rahall feared both mother and son and he had much respect for *la padrona's* judgment if not so much for Ramon'.

It was a mystery to most how Maria Pacheco got where she was. Rahall thought she'd come out of the Juarez slums, daughter of a *puta* and likely one herself, once. Maria claimed her mother was killed by a drunken off-duty policeman, and she hated every cop she saw. She had worked in a Juarez nightclub and she had Ramon by the owner, who dealt in drugs, guns, porn, young flesh and break-your-bones. When her lover carelessly lost his head in an argument with a rival with a machete, Maria took over managing the club and had three more children by another short-lived father. She seemed to prosper with each mate's demise, which probably didn't catch her completely by surprise. Much of this history was only rumor among her minions. How she got to southern Colorado with her hands in firm control of a criminal syndicate, none of them had been around long enough to know. It wasn't a business that valued employment stability and few had been enlisted for more than a few years. The Pachecos did not explain much and when they did of course they lied.

Rahall had risen to be their collector for a network of 20 dealers because he did not question what Pachecos told him or wanted done. He was happy in his job but in fact his career trajectory showed signs of droop.

"I could visit him," he suggested next. "See if he's got it together."

"Are you loco?" Maria spit the question. "Stay the fuck away from him. You don't go near a jail. You drive by it you don't even look at it. He gets out, you stay away from him until we check out everything."

She stared hard at the *tonto*. He had been one of her best men, strong, savvy, not bad looking. It was evident now that he was using. He was down twenty pounds at least, he smelled sour and kept licking dry lips. There was a patch of whiskers on his chin he'd missed shaving, another scrim of hairs forming just under his nose that the blade had missed, a blob of orangey wax in his left ear. She held her expression bland even as she was coming to a decision about him.

"Understand me?"

Rahall nodded and couldn't meet her eyes. He looked at his knees and then out the side window.

She hit the Toyota's door handle and slid her short legs out the door. Looking back in she said, "Be back here for me in one hour."

She stepped off in the noon glare, red leather purse in one hand and a shopping bag in the other, somebody's grandma doing errands.

Rahall watched her for half a block, hating the bitch and trusting it didn't show. He put the car in gear and eased away from the curb, on a short route to the first slug of feel-good he could find.

"Tirado. He's our key."

Tanner looked around at the other men in the room, Groton his RAC, Ben Hayden, who'd survived the gunfight unscathed, and two DEA agents who'd be consulting on narcotics aspects of the investigation and reinforcing on stings, Harry Thornell and Bill Caputo.

Tanner had been checking Tirado out of jail and bringing him into the office in handcuffs and leg shackles to work at a corkboard, making an organizational chart of the Pacheco organization. Tanner told the informant to give up everybody he knew above him and all of those down to two levels below. Sometimes Tirado could give only a street name and often wasn't sure of an address.

With each new name, Tanner went to the drug squads and intelligence units of the Colorado Springs and Fountain police departments and checked it against their Field Interview Reports. These are three-by-five cards officers fill out every time they make a street arrest, writing down information on the vehicle as well as names and addresses of everyone also in the car. When he verified an identity, Tanner added the names of everyone who'd previously been found with him to that suspect's box on the chart. When Tirado knew only a street name, sometimes the local police could provide a complete identity based on their previous contacts.

At the end of each day before taking Tirado back to the lockup, Tanner helped him slip a raincoat over his orange jail jumpsuit, topped him off with sunglasses and hat and drove him around until he recognized an address where he'd done meth transactions. Tanner had a tape recorder on the seat beside him and as they rolled by he read out the make and model of the vehicles in the driveway and dictates a description of the house. If Tirado ever had been inside the property, Tanner had him draw a diagram of the rooms. When it came time to execute search warrants, he wanted no surprises.

"So far what he's giving me checks out," Tanner told the team. "Over the last two weeks I've gotten forty-five individuals who appear to be significant operators in Pacheco meth distribution. We may turn up more, and some of these we have now could fade on us."

Every agent in the room knew that a criminal conspiracy often had no clearly defined limits and poking into one was almost sure to lead to as many frustrations as eureka's, with characters coming on scene and disappearing as quickly, and their relationships understood only to each other if to anyone at all. Many were, after all, marinading brain cells in chemicals that burned the enamel off teeth, and their reliability would vary day to day. And if their operation could be pulled apart, some could slip away to reappear later and try to build another network.

"I have a line on Ramon, the one the Crips said they dealt guns with," said Tanner. "Tirado says his *Capitan* is Ramon Pacheco who is very close to the person at the top. Get this, it's a woman, Ramon' mother, name of Maria Pacheco."

The agents took a minute to think about that, knowing the management skill needed for keeping drug dealers obedient. Hayden said, "Not sure I can picture a mom like that."

"What I'm told, she's still something of a looker if you like a double handful," said Tanner. "Dresses well, lives quietly, modest home, is driven around in an old car. Has grandchildren in Mexico, shows off pictures of them. But, Tirado tells me his people try very hard to see only that side of her."

As described by Tirado, Maria Pacheco operated on a front system. She had four guys who took a pound or two of processed meth from her every other day, agreeing to pay her back at an agreed price of up to $10,000 per pound. Each of them had ten or fifteen buyers who were advanced a quarter pound that they broke into ounces at $1,200 per. That was her wholesale staff. Below that and looking to work their way up were buyers taking a half-ounce, an eighth-ounce called eight-balls at $300 and down to sixteenths, called teeners, for $125. All the way down to the lower levels the product was advanced on the promise of payback.

The money came back up the chain and Maria Pacheco collected between $100,000 and $150,000 every other day. Upwards of twenty-two million dollars a year, she made it with virtually no overhead costs. The ATF didn't know that yet because Tirado had no certain knowledge of where the Pachecos got their raw materials and cooked the meth. Tirado only knew the distribution. To discover the manufacturing end of it, Tanner had to get inside.

It took two weeks to verify Tirado's story name by name. By then Tanner figured he had earned the ten percent down payment for the bondsman to post his $15,000 bail.

"So you're going to bond him out tomorrow," Groton said leaning back in his chair. "Then what?"

"We begin getting me into some part of the group."

"Watch yourself. These things get tricky," Groton told his younger agent. "Trust him?"

"The same as most. It's the risk I take."

Every man in the room already knew both sides of the conversation these two were having, each knowing the other's questions and the other's response before asked and answered. It was, though, the conversation to have before every agent went undercover, the ritual. Each one would be haunted if they didn't run through the cautionary queries and reassurances, and an agent got complacent and things went bad.

All knew that working confidential informants was one of the most challenging aspects of the job. Some agents shied away from it because missteps could damage careers or lead to dismissal, even jail. Some who tried it ended up getting sucked into the web of the informant, who wound up twisting the investigation. Groton once warned Tanner, "Never trust anyone who doesn't have as much to loose as you." Tanner had always reasoned that those willing to betray best buddies and family members couldn't be trusted at all, and it would be only a matter of time before they tried to work both sides, or confessed to friends or lovers what they were doing, got scared and split.

"Just so long as you know and you're ready," Groton said. "This shitbird is probably going to try and fuck you."

"Yes sir, he will. But first I'll make him take me to the prom."

5

Richard Tirado squinted in the parking lot glare as he walked out of the windowless jail and sniffed deep through his nose. "Oh man," he said, turning to the fat bondsman who'd just posted his bail, "that place smells so bad I don't know how you can keep going in there."

Abe Glick looked his client over like he was considering something on his shoe. "Well Mr. Tirado, it's an ugly job but somebody's got to do it. That's frequently me. And you'll appreciate it's a business that just keeps on giving, thanks to the repeat customers in there. That's often you. So my advice is, hold your sensitive nose and go fuck yourself while I go to the bank." Glick took his client tightly by the arm and led his wayward ass to a dented Honda sedan parked in the lot's one shady corner. "A little more business to conduct."

Tanner, sitting behind the wheel, gestured for both to get in the car. He reached in his briefcase and pulled out an envelope with $5,000 and passed it over the backrest to Tirado on the rear seat.

"Now you pass the money to Mr. Glick."

Tirado passed the cash back to Glick in the front, completing charade and legality.

Tanner turned to the bondsman, "Sid, anyone asks, Mister Tirado here paid his own bail. We're clear on that, right?"

"As a summer day."

They shook hands and Glick got out, the car rising as he did, and climbed into his Lincoln, his bulk sinking it by a couple inches, bestowing a regal wave as he slowly drove away.

Tirado demanded now, "So what do I say why it took so long to post bond, if I paid it myself?"

"Say you have an aunt in Austin who lent you the money, and give her name. Anybody wants to call to verify, give this number. It feeds into a special phone relay we have set up in our office wired to an Austin area code, and it will be answered by your dear old aunt who happens to be an ATF secretary with acting experience. Anybody calls at night, an answering machine with her voice on it will pick up the call."

"Time to get to work," Tanner said, reaching into the briefcase and lifting out a one-watt transmitter. "Take off your shirt."

Tirado looked alarmed. "They find me with that, I'm dead in the desert."

"Here's the plan," Tanner said, "you don't let 'em search you. Just say no. I mean that. Don't let anybody punk you."

He taped the little device to Tirado's side just under his arm. "Now you're going to see your girlfriend."

Tammy Chisholm was a meth head and occasional dating escort who Tirado said was a go-between for the Pachecos. Tanner had cruised her home and hangouts and observed she was a slender elaborately tattooed blond with musical notes inked along her neck and shoulders and butterflies up the backs of her legs. Aside from her album of tramp stamps, which Tanner ranked with nose studs as a turn-on, Chisholm was an eye-catcher but maybe not itch free where the butterflies headed.

Tirado had claimed he and Chisholm were not really hooked up but he wasn't convincing, and just in case Tanner advised him, "Don't be taking off your shirt. Just your pants."

It got him a slight smile and a shake of the head.

"Tell her you've got to get somewhere else and you want a gun for protection. You say the cops grabbed the load you were delivering and you need to be strapped."

The agent handed $1,200 in small bills. "Count it and sign this receipt."

"What for?" Tirado asked. "I trust you"

"That's nice. I'll inform Washington. Now count the cash and sign for it. The money's for a gun and dope — just a little score at first. Remember, you've just bonded out so you're pinched. Don't push it. Let her do most of the talking, try to find out what's been going on while you were in the slam."

Tanner handed over the keys to Tirado's pickup and pointed to where it was parked across the lot next to the exit. He explained he'd taped a repeater to the seatback to kick out the signal so he could park away from the meet and still get good sound from the transmitter under Tirado's armpit.

"You try to keep your mind off the wire. Just know I'm listening and I'm close if there's any trouble."

Now he put his hands on Tirado's shoulders and pulled him close, locking eyes. "Don't think you are smarter than me. Don't fuck with me in any shape or fashion. Don't."

His informant nodded and Tanner let him go. "I'll give you forty-five minutes to get in and get out and to bring me what you buy and the money you do not spend. After that I will come in there and get you! Understood? Alright, let's ride."

The F-150 stopped on a street of small homes and weedy yards, and Tirado trudged across a lawn unmown this summer past a black late model Sebring convertible in the driveway.

Tanner, parked half a block down, watched as Chisholm opened the door almost immediately and pulled Tirado inside. The sounds of a grapple and mouth-lock came across the wire.

What Tanner can hear:

"Easy, babe. I been slammed so long I wouldn't get past (unintelligible) your hand right now. I've got to get back to Fountain to check some things (unintelligible) back later tonight if I can."

Sounds of clothes rustling.

". . . action been good?"

"Ramon (unintelligible) on top of things (unintelligible) said Maria was worried about you but (tape hissing) would be better for you to get out of this on your own."

"My aunt in Austin came through with the bail. I'm going to ask the organization to reimburse her."

"Sure . . . You want a jolt of something?"

"Not now. Tell me what's been happening."

"We're cooking and moving the product quickly. Maria and Ramon are worried about Rahall. He's strung out much of the time . . . making (unintelligible) decisions."

"*Like what?*"

"*Ramon says Maria thinks he probably would have hit you just to make sure you weren't talking to Feds (unintelligible) stirred up a shit storm. Rahall's hanging with some bikers Maria thinks would love to muscle in. Maria has warned him. Ramon said your cut would keep so long as you kept your mouth shut. I said no one was tighter lipped or more into this than you (tape hissing).*"

"*I have to get down to Fountain. You have any crystal? I'll pay. Oh yeah. If you have a spare piece, I could use that for (tape hissing) cops took my hardware.*"

"*(unintelligible) ounce for nine hundred. Here. Let you have the Smith .38. (tape hissing) a hundred and fifty.*"

Sounds of clothes rustling, breathing.

"*(unintelligible) this and I'll be here for days. Really got to go.*"

"*Coming back later?*"

"*If I can .*"

Tirado didn't look around for Tanner when he came out. He got in the truck and burned rubber, turning right at the first intersection and driving more than a mile before he pulled over and waited.

Tanner pulled alongside and motioned for him to follow. They drove to a strip mall and around to the back, where Tanner parked and walked quickly to Tirado's truck before he could get out. He stood back of the cab.

"Give me the piece."

"I might need it."

"Yeah, but you paid her for it and its evidence now. Besides, I catch you carrying I'll put you so far back in the jail they'll have to shoot your beans through a tube. And let's have the dope and remaining cash."

Tirado handed over the revolver. Tanner looked at the crystal and thought, this is really fresh, then pocketed it and counted the bills.

"Nine hundred for the dope, hundred fifty for the gun, leaves two bills. Not bad for your first time, though a little short on conversation. Let me have the recorder."

Tirado looked around at the empty lot, reaching into his shirt and gingerly unsticking the tape from his chest. He handed over the wire along with the repeater from behind the seat, and as he did his gut rumbled loud enough for both to hear.

"Hungry?" Tanner asked. "Follow me." He got back into his car and drove to the front of the mall, parking in front of Piazza's Pizza that turned out to be a not-real-clean and poorly lighted place. They took the booth at the back. It was two in the afternoon and except for an old man at a front table they were the only customers. Tirado ordered a medium sausage with double cheese and Tanner said he'd just have a slice.

When their waitress sashayed away, Tanner said, "You did good back there."

The informant looked around and leaned over the table, his head bowed so the words were low. "There was something too cozy going on. I mean we've had some nice times but she was acting almost like I'm her long lost boyfriend. I'm thinking, what the fuck does she know here, am I being set up?"

"First time jitters," Tanner said.

"Easy enough for you to say. How do I defend myself if it comes to that?"

"No gun, Richard. But I've got to tell you there are risks. You have to decide whether it's worth it not to be spending most of the rest of your life in prison."

They shut up when the waitress, who both noticed had a curvy behind and tomato sauce on her apron, brought their cokes and pizza. Tanner's first bite was surprisingly good and he figured this place had to make his short list of the good and dirty.

"Now you're getting me into the action," Tanner said when she wriggled away.

"I can't walk you right in, for fuck's sake!"

"No. What we do is give you ten days of freedom. Then you introduce me around as a buddy from Kansas who happens to be a gun guy and meth dealer. We've got prison records fixed for me there if anybody checks."

Tirado looked fatigued at the prospect of what was ahead.

"Go home to Fountain," Tanner said. "Get some sleep and then make contact with Ramon. Here's an untraceable throwaway cell phone. At 3 p.m. tomorrow I want you to call 388-2424 and leave a message for your Aunt that you got the package and hang up. You meet me one hour later right here.

Tanner reached out to shake his informant's hand, pressing two hundred dollar bills into his palm. "Good job. You earned this." He paid the check and left without looking back.

Tirado took another ten minutes to finish eating, left a $5 tip from the $100 Tanner had given him as walking around money on the table and headed for the door.

"Have a nice day," said the waitress, smiling as he passed the cash register. He didn't hear her. He was thinking, by sunup he could be in Mexico. Then he thought, if the Pachecos thought he'd run because he'd given them up, he wouldn't be safe there either. The big fed wouldn't be so hard to handle down there, but he could put bad talk on him here, and the border didn't mean shit to the Pachecos.

6

Mother and son sat at her kitchen table in Fountain having a late night coffee and discussing a once-valued employee who might have to make a career move. They knew it would mean the death of him.

"Rahall's always strung out," Maria Pacheco said. "I don't think we can afford to have a man doing distribution who is also a heavy user."

Her son agreed. He'd dropped by Rahall's pad yesterday and seen his eyeballs like pinpoints and hands twitching, the place reeking cat piss, while two skinny women walked around in underpants, toking up. He described the scene to his mother, and because he was weary lapsed into Spanish, "*Si, mamacita, ya es hora de que haya terminado.*" Yawning, he added, "But who replaces him?"

"I've been thinking about that. Tirado is out on bond. Maybe he moves up."

Ramon Pacheco got up to top up his coffee, saw it was midnight on the clock and put the cup in the sink. He didn't like the idea. "I'm thinking maybe both should go."

"Well, there is no indication Richard cooperated with police. He stayed in too long for that. He got a relative to send money for the bond. I think we use him but keep an eye on him. He could take over Rahall's distributors and maybe help you with collections. I have not decided this, just thinking."

Ramon knew he could use help pulling in money owed but he didn't think Tirado had the *cojones* for the work. While the Pachecos had a desirable product and their business model was otherwise excellent, their clientele plainly lacked class. The irony, Ramon well understood, was that the more devoted the customers the more unreliable, and so the more need for pay-up pressure on them. As you went down the supply chain, buyer assets diminished because no meth-head had any job for long. Tweakers ultimately had few income options beyond thieving and renting their private parts to strangers.

Something every cop knows, though few civilians seem aware of, is that drug addict's account for nearly all burglaries in America. They steal four things almost exclusively – cash, or jewelry and guns and computers that have a ready cash value. So the Pachecos had caches of hundreds of stolen weapons in residences through eastern Colorado, which became another highly profitable line of inventory for their Arms "R" Us subsidiary. They did not accept computers or jewels for payment, and tweakers had to find their own buyers for these commodities to get money for their next fix.

A problem for Maria and Ramon was the propensity of dollars to stick to every change of hand. They could not tolerate shortchanging by subordinates and borrowers and still remain in control of their own enterprise. The questions they had trouble answering tonight were whether Tirado was the right one to succeed Rahall in making collections, and if not who was there?

Midnight passed with Tomas Rahall stretched back on his purple velvet couch, sucking on his meth pipe and feeling no pain when a spark from the bowl fell on his bare belly. Two of his runners and four women also sprawled around the living room, each looking in need of home cooking and familiarity with showers. Their bodies and faces advertised a phenomenon experienced by hard users, that interest in food and hygiene fades even as meth stimulates appetites for sex. An outcome of this was the certain conjugation of the very horny with the really skanky.

To imagine wider options than they really had, tonight they had their eyes on a sixty-inch plasma TV that showed in high resolution and amazing magnification a tangle of moaning porn stars as naked as themselves but actually, to appearances, rather more wholesome.

"It doesn't get any better than this," said Rahall. He ran a hand lightly over the breast of a woman to his right and repeated himself, "It doesn't get any better than this." When she didn't answer, her attention held by pixilated close-up of a penis as big on the screen as a human leg, he asked, "You think it gets any better than this?" Not getting quick enough reply, Rahall stood up and said her, "I'll be right back, you wanna see something better than this."

He walked down a narrow hall, past other rooms where guests were exploring limits of pharmacology, felt over a door jam for a key and opened the metal door to a supply closet. He put his hand on a stainless .357, thinking he should have kept it handier from the start.

The party shouldn't really be here, he knew that but he didn't care. This was a drop house of the Pacheco's, the deed registered to a name on a gravestone. The trailer park manager regularly got envelopes of cash under his door to overlook anything out of the ordinary going on here. Nobody lived here. No one ordinarily came here until late at night, and then they stopped their cars outside the park and walked to the trailer and did their business quietly.

Tirado knew if Maria heard about his orgy tonight, she'd be murderous. *Fuck her and the burro she rode across the river.* He had an exit plan.

The day was done and the next one beginning when Tanner rolled up I-25 toward the Douglas County line and his home on five sweet acres. There, in the kitchen he found a foil-covered plate containing dinner now hours old. He was putting it back in the fridge when Sally, in slippers, came up behind and surprised him with a hug.

"I woke up, heard your car. So how's my gumshoe tonight."

He turned into her arms and bent his head to the bend of her neck, inhaling a scent fresh and earthy, no, herby, something like marjoram. He held her while he let go of the day.

"This is the start of some things," he told her. "It means long and late hours." He waited a beat, "Probably some undercover work."

He could feel Sally tense. Since the shootout she'd become edgier when discussing his work, though she made no demands.

"No big worries in it," he said, conviction in his voice. "Most of it is going to be handled by a confidential informant. I'll be in and out of cover and mostly on the fringe."

She heard the lie and then she kissed him.

Insistent ringing of the phone jolted Tanner awake. He focused fuzzily on the digital clock, 1:30 a.m. Sally mumbled in irritation and turned toward the wall.

"Sam? Jim Sanderson in Fountain."

"Hey chief," he said.

"That case you're working? Involves a Tomas Rahall?"

Uh-oh. Tanner hesitated, preparing for bad news sure to come at this hour.

"Yeah."

"Well he's dead."

"Shit!" Tanner said. He put his hand over the receiver as Sally raised her head. "It's okay, babe," he told her. "One of our suspects in a case has been killed. Go back to sleep." Fat chance of that, he thought, turning back to the voice on the phone.

"He was shot at a trailer park the north end of town," Sanderson said. "You'll want to see this."

On clear roads it took him only forty-five minutes to the trailer park, where occupants had been drawn outside by the blue flashing lights of patrol cars parked in front of a mobile home disreputable even among the fifteen other shabby metal boxes.

Entering, he could see across the room a long body with rivulet of blood from its head soaking into the gold pile carpet. A big revolver lay a few feet from the victim's right hand.

Chief Sanderson and his top detective, LaForce, stood over the corpse. Leaning casually in a corner, his arms folded, was Colorado Springs patrolman Tyler Rush who'd been assigned to liaison with ATF. Tanner had called Rush before leaving home and the younger officer lived closer and had beaten him to the scene. They exchanged a look of understanding. Since the shootout in the Springs and his chief's run-n with Tanner, Rush had been officially assigned to foster better relations between CPSD and the federal agency. His covert mission was to keep Chief Beetle appraised of what ATF was investigating. The mistrust had sprung from activities of the Crips, who peddled their coke in the Springs during the week with little hassle and went home weekends crowing about the lameness of CSPD compared to enforcement they knew in Compton and East LA. Tanner was fully aware of Rush's role but he liked the officer and believed he wouldn't tell his bosses everything he learned the feds were doing. Rush had proved his discretion several times, so Tanner had rung him out of courtesy.

"Anything obvious here?" Tanner asked. "Aside from a dead guy on the floor?"

He leaned over for a look at the bullet hole in the upturned cheek. It had powder tattooing and he turned the head to better see a large hole at the back. It indicated the bullet fired at close range entered at an upward angle under his left eye. Rahall seemed to have leaned forward and slipped off the couch after the shot and then rolled onto his right side.

"Only one problem. . ." answered LaForce, waiting for Tanner to catch it.

He did. "How does a right-handed man shoot himself in the left cheek at that angle, especially with a hog leg this large. If it indeed is the murder weapon?"

"Yup." the detective agreed. "It looks, maybe, like someone tried to set this up to look like suicide."

All four officers tried pointing right forefingers at their own left cheeks, straining to get the angle correct.

"He couldn't have done this himself," Rush insisted.

"Maybe not," said Tanner, less sure. "Coroner on the way?"

"Yes," the chief said. "He lives a ways out and I told him not to rush. We have the lab guys also on the way."

"Did anyone outside see anything?"

LaForce answered, "Several residents heard the shot and saw people running from the trailer, a couple of them toting satchels. We logged the call about the gunshot two hours ago. It came from a payphone at the front of the property and one of the neighbors admits making it.

"Rahall would have used this place for a distribution center," Tanner noted. "Have you found anything much?

"Nada," the chief said. "The lab boys might come up with drug traces, probably will in fact. The place was littered with bottles and even smoldering cigarettes in the ashtrays. We figure maybe six or eight people here when Tirado was shot. We did find a crack pipe on the couch, warm. Anything of value likely was in those satchels the tweaks ran with."

Tanner turned to Rush. "Listen, someone has to get over to Tirado's real home and lock down the place. God knows what he has over there. If this is Maria Pacheco's handiwork, the place is going to be ransacked before we know it. I'm heading there now. Chief, we need somebody putting the search warrants in motion, if that's all right with you."

"That's a plan," Sanderson replied.

Tanner smiled his thanks. "We'll make sure you're informed as we go, and you do the same. I really appreciate the call and the help with this. Who knows where it leads?"

Tanner sat in his government car two doors down from the yellow clapboard house Tomas Rahall had called home and watched as friends of the deceased showed how much they cared. Detective LaForce sat in his squad car parked across the street, watching too, and looking over at Tanner to wipe away a pretend tear.

It was 3 a.m. and Rahall's front yard was full of his social set. Being out at that hour wasn't so unusual for tweakers, who routinely stayed up four and five days at a time in frenetic action, but rarely did they show this unity of purpose. They had formed a bucket brigade from the front door to a silver SUV at the curb and were passing momentos of their friend one to another -- a television . . . a computer . . . another TV . . . . a cardboard box of paperwork, apparently . . . a rifle . . . a rifle . . . a rifle . . . another computer . . . an armful of clothes . . . a shotgun . . . a two-drawer filing cabinet . . .

For a guy who died naked in a shit box house trailer, Tanner reflected, he sure left a lot of stuff to remember him by.

LaForce leaned his head out his car window, "We don't want to break this up yet, do we?"

Tanner grinned, "Oh no. Not when these concerned citizens are collecting all this evidence for us in a convenient place."

When the SUV looked nearly full and the passing of goodies from the house seemed to be slowing, the two officers got out of their cars and walked up to within fifteen feet of the line of loaders, where they stood unnoticed. Tanner spoke in normal volume, "You recognize any of these people, Vince?"

"Are you kidding? Right here's the pond scum of the gene pool in Fountain, Colorado." LaForce was pointing to individuals as he spoke and still wasn't noticed.

Tanner walked to the SUV and tapped the shoulder of a waif in a tank top and flip flops. "Hi there," said Tanner, "what are you all doing?"

Without looking up, she said, "Tomas is dead. We got to clean out the house before the cops get here."

"Oh I see. Not a bad idea. Except they're already here." He stuck his federal badge under her nose."

For the five seconds it took to process his words, she said nothing, then shouted, "Cops," and made a break for the house. Everyone in the line dropped their bundles and began running in different directions, some crashing through a hedge at the far side of the yard, some colliding and falling down, some bumping into arriving patrolmen who grabbed and dragged them back to the house.

"You take over inside and I'll secure the car," Tanner said. He called Rush and told him to include a warrant for the SUV. When extra officers arrived, they began to inventory everything dropped in the yard and log it as abandoned property and evidence in a crime.

When he walked into the house a half hour later, Tanner found LaForce sitting on a chair in the middle of a room bathed in blue and red lights and full of cigarette smoke. Arrayed on the floor around him were members of the "bucket brigade" that the uniforms had managed to collar. LaForce excused himself politely to the group, told them "Please remain sitting," got up and led Tanner back out to the front porch so they could share a laugh.

"Looked like you're teaching some kind of class in there" Tanner said. "On substance abuse?"

"More like group therapy," said LaForce. "We were just getting to know one another and you'd be surprised at all the things I'm finding out."

"You didn't learn who drives that SUV, did you?" Tanner said he was headed to the police department lot to inspect the loot inside it and needed to take whoever it belonged to with him.

LaForce stepped to the doorway and called, "Sharon."

"Sharon?" Tanner said. "Jeez Vince, you really are good. How long have you known this woman?"

"Only about fifteen minutes but I'm a highly skilled interrogator, and I've learned how to get people go give up their secrets. There's one or two other things about her I've discovered that'll prove significant when you're driving her in."

"Like?"

"Like she needs a bath."

Tanner drove her to the station with the windows down. After he bought her a coke and took her to the interview room, she told him her name was Sharon Sunday, she was nineteen, and the SUV was registered to her mother. And mom, it turned out, was more upset to be awakened by a call from a cop than to learn her daughter was in jail. "I was asleep," she protested. "She's always doing something." When the woman demanded to know when she could get her vehicle, Tanner was pleased to advise her it was evidence for now and she should look for a new ride. Leaving Sharon with her coke and the jitters, he went to find Rush, who had typed up warrants and put in a call to a state magistrate on duty. When the warrants were faxed back, the two walked outside to the impound lot to check the SUV for Rahall's belongings.

It was 6:30 a.m. when Tanner and Rush opened up the SUV and found twenty semi-automatic weapons, three sawed-off shotguns, a box with $10,000 in cash, a jug containing phenol 2 propanol, the main ingredient in manufacturing meth, along with enough electronic gadgetry to stock a pawnshop.

"I'd like to be watching when the Pachecos hear about this," said Rush.

"Yeah, I'd say they're having considerable consternation. But what I'd rather be witnessing is what they do when they get done with their tantrums. There's going to be a big corporate shake-up, and when we know which way it's going we can exploit it."

"How?"

"Easy. I was a business major."

Rush took in the gun on his belt, the jeans, scuffed cowboy boots, the big rough hands, scar on his chin and the wayward nose that had plainly known adversity. "Where'd you go wrong?"

"Was probably my people skills. That principle the customer is always right just isn't me. I'm better suited for a line of work where everybody understands the customers are almost always wrong. The ones I'm happiest serving are those I can tell, 'You have the right to remain silent.'"

7

"What the hell is going on? Rahall is dead!"

Tirado's voice on the phone came as practically a shout in his ear. Tanner moved his cell an inch away. "Where are you?"

"I'm in the car headed for Fountain."

"Where have you been? How do you know about Rahall?"

"Wait a minute," Tirado said. "Are you trying to implicate me in this? "Should   I   be?"

"Christ no. Goddamn it, I'm smarter than that. When the sonofabitch was high he was crazy and I always tried to keep away from him then. I was at Tammy's. I told you I was going back there for a date to put off any suspicion. She got a call around midnight and when she hung up she was white as a sheet. She said the call was from Ramon Pacheco and someone had shot Rahall."

"That's what she said? Somebody shot Rahall?"

"Absolutely, and that Maria was calling a meeting for tomorrow and to tell me I was supposed to be there."

"What time's the meeting and where?"

"It's eight tomorrow night, at a place that Maria owns between Fountain and Pueblo, the deep boonies. What should I do?"

"Okay," Tanner said. "Here's what you do. Go home. If he calls you there you should be there. I'll be here past noon on this thing. I want you to call me about one o'clock and I'll have instructions. I don't want to meet you here. The Pachecos have too many eyes."

Tanner hung up, left the building and ran through a downpour to his car. When he got to Rahall's house he found only LaForce, who said none of the people they'd detained there had been at the trailer or witnessed the shooting.

"They just hang out around Rahall like disciples," LaForce said. "That's what they were doing tonight. An older guy they had seen around several times before showed up and told them of Rahall's death and said the place needed to be cleaned out. This guy was carrying a briefcase. He took it into a back bedroom, came back out quickly and left."

One thing LaForce said he had discovered was Rahall worked for a powerful woman and actually was one of her main collectors.

"If he was a collector, it meant he probably also was her muscle and gun supplier," Tanner said. "If somebody goes bad on a debt, it is up to him to put it right at whatever cost and that means some violence. A guy like that would have some enemies."

The detective nodded. "Yeah, well my notes from these guys are just full of rumors and suspicions about who killed him, including someone they called Pacheco who is connected to the woman. One of the men said Rahall got drunk one night and expressed some fear of this guy. Maybe we should bring him in and find out who the woman is."

"To be honest with you," Tanner said, not wanting to be completely honest with him, "We're in the midst of an investigation that may involve this Pacheco person and I don't want to compromise it. We should hold off on him for the time being and see where other angles lead us."

It was a tricky position to take. The last thing Tanner wanted to do is alienate the local police. From Tirado he'd learned more about Rahall's higher-ups than the locals knew yet, but it could jeopardize his informant to reveal it too soon. But the Fountain cops knew more about Rahall and his street action than he did and would be of help in the bigger picture.

"Seems to me that none of this is a surprise to you," said LaForce, locking eyes. "You've been working hard since we last spoke a couple of weeks ago. You can't tell me more about it?"

"Not yet. Soon. You have my word."

The two began searching the house. It took only a few minutes to discover more drugs and weapons, but no more money.

"We could have put this guy away for a long time," Tanner said. "My guess is that he had a lot more money in here than we've come up with and the old guy your kids saw took most of it out in the briefcase."

Tanner said he was on his way back to Colorado Springs to get a few hours of sleep and would be back down by early evening. He reported that the girl, Sharon, was belligerent and LaForce could deal with her.

"I don't think she's much of anything except a small timer and user. If she knows anything, she'll tell you before me. I Mirandized her just to be on the safe side and called her mother. The apple didn't fall far from that tree. See you tomorrow."

The rain had eased up considerably when Tanner climbed into his car at 1 p.m. and headed for the Interstate. To keep awake on the drive home he pulled up at a truck stop on I-25 for coffee and put in a call to Tirado.

"I want you to go to the meeting tomorrow and act like you're ready and able to take over for Rahall," he told the informant. "I'll contact you Monday morning with further instructions."

Tirado had just one question, "Who killed Rahall?"

"I don't know. Maybe Ramon. Maria had to be worried about the strung-out bastard and she might be cleaning house. Take care, but I don't think there is anything you have to be concerned about. I have a feeling someone else got to him before they did." He broke off the call.

During the drive home Tanner couldn't help feel that something was missing. If Rahall had been shot by anyone in the trailer at the time, they should have had a line on it quickly. But the position of the body and the way the shot had entered made it seem certain that someone had pulled the trigger on Maria's man. If it wasn't one of Maria's people how did they know so quickly to order a cleanup attempt at Rahall's residence? None of those at the house had been at the trailer, at least according to what LaForce had discovered and he was a perceptive interviewer. One thing seemed certain. Rahall's death would both leave a void in Maria's organization and cause a great deal of confusion that he felt he could exploit.

"*Jesus Christo*! What went on out there?"

Maria Pacheco furious, and afraid that the business she had built up over fifteen years, her control of a meth market that reached from Colorado to California, was heading for collapse.

"Mama, I don't know," Ramon said. "I expected to find Rahall at the trailer by himself. I would have handled it quietly. But when I arrived there was a lot of noise and a bunch of cars."

He shook his head at his mother and sat down heavily in a chair. "I was sitting in my car for a minute, thinking it over, when suddenly people are running from the trailer like it was on fire. There were at least five including two of our distributors. I would have gone into the trailer to check, but the people who live out there were coming out of their places because of the commotion. I knew the cops must have been notified."

Ramon paused for a breath and Maria raged at him, "You know this is trouble for us. That son of a bitch also was renting a house that I own. What do we do about that?"

"As his landlord, you had no idea. Nobody can prove any different. I called Manny and told him to get the hell over to the house and secure the money. There are always a number of bums hanging about but they're loyal to Rahall, and Manny was to tell them to begin cleaning out the place before any cops show up."

"So?"

"He got there and found the money Rahall owed us. There coulda been more but he didn't have time to look around. He told a girl there to look for that canvas bag Rahall used for collections and if she found it to pitch it in the back of her car along with everything else. Of course if she opens it and finds cash, forget it. But Manny had to get the hell out of there."

"He better be showing up here soon."

Maria considered Manny Suarez the one indispensable man in her organization. Though he didn't have an active role in the distribution of product or collection of money, he was, she knew, more important to her survival than her own son. Manny ran her errands, he listened to her worries, he gave the very best advice, and when she felt in danger it was Manny she turned to. Maria had known him since she was a child on the streets of Juarez, and when she was grown and moving into the drug trade, he had kept her safe. Manny Suarez had come to the states on a work visa that Maria had bought for him through an officer in the old Immigration and Naturalization Service. Now he performed odd jobs for her and sometimes drove her around. Even though he was about to turn seventy he was, still, the surest killer she knew. He was also her lover.

"How much did Manny find?"

"A little over a hundred grand."

It seemed to appease her. "That's about right for a week's collections. At least Rahall wasn't skimming us." She went behind the bar and poured a shot of tequila, an indulgence she rarely allowed herself. "Now who the hell shot him?"

"God knows," her son replied. "He had enemies, every collector does."

"Have you reached Tirado?"

"Yeah, finally, at home. I told him about Rahall and he sounded shocked. He said he had been with Tammy. I had already called her and told her and that she had not mentioned him being there. He told me he had left before she got the call and that she was probably overwhelmed and frightened by the news. He said he would be at the meeting this evening."

"He'll have to take over Rahall's section."

"Suppose so," Ramon said. "For the time being. See if he works out."

"Let's try him." She put her hand over his on the bar and squeezed, and he nearly winced. She was a strong woman. "I want you to cover our tracks in this. It would take sheer luck or a genius to link the trailer to us, but find a way to burn the thing. As for the house, Manny cleans up the place and puts it in the hands of a rental agent. It's the best I can do."

She knew the police would have a hard time buying her lack of knowledge about Rahall's activities, but she didn't see how they could prove it. She worried about the Feds coming into it, but told herself this was just a local shooting and they'd likely chalk it up to a small time dealer. But maybe not. Maybe the killer had done them a favor. Maybe it was time to get out. She had a fortune in banks in Mexico and a numbered account in Switzerland. She would talk to Manny. Ramon wouldn't want to walk away from the business. Maybe she would just let him have it. But she would talk to Manny, that was what to do."

"Get out of here," she told her son. "I need to think."

Maria was painting her toenails when Manny's big Chrysler rumbled up the driveway. He smiled when he came in the back door and saw what she was doing. He pulled up a footstool and sat, reaching for the little brush. "I do that for you."

It got to her, as it always did, when the man with no sympathy for others was tender with her. He did now what he did so well, he listened as she talked, nodding, or raising an eyebrow or squinting an eye when he might disagree. Her thoughts cleared. Maria decided that at the meeting tonight she would tell her people she was giving her son more authority. From now on they would take direct orders from him, not her. She would say that Tirado would replace Rahall and that he would work with Tammy Chisholm.

As she explained her plan to Manny, he suggested a timetable, six to nine months at most for getting out. Meantime, he said, the rest of the organization should believe things were going as usual. He would make certain that if anyone got out of line, they got back in it. "Or I make them gone."

"*Esto es bueno,*" she told him.

The meeting went smoothly. Tirado accepted the new assignment but surprised them with some reservation.

"This is temporary. I don't want the job forever—just long enough to make some money get the hell out of here. I can't leave my aunt high and dry after putting up bond and I need a wad to set me up somewhere else."

After the meeting, he left with Tammy and headed for a late hours club in Colorado Springs. "I want a big score," he told her. "I will do it for a while but something tells me I don't have a future in management."

8

Three days after the shooting Tanner was alone in the Colorado Springs office, filling in paperwork describing Rahall's death, when the phone rang. A woman who sounded young and scared and said her name was Jane Compton asked to come in and speak to him. She said she knew things about the incident and wanted to get out of town, but she didn't want anybody tracking her down when she did. She wanted to explain.

A half hour later the buzzer on the outer door went off. The young woman outside the glass entrance stood nervously shifting her weight one foot to the other. He let her in, picking the purse off her shoulder by the strap before she could protest, opened it quickly and peered inside. Finding no weapon he handed it back. When he led her into the interview room, she perched on the edge of her seat.

"What is this about?"

She said the word was on the street that police were trying to find who murdered Rahall. "It wasn't murder, it was suicide. I saw it. I was right there."

"Okay, let me see some ID."

She reached in her purse and brought out her Colorado driver's license and handed it to him. Jane Compton was twenty-five, five-foot-eight, a hundred and fifteen pounds with brown eyes and brown hair. She lived on Butte Street in Fountain. He handed the license back to her.

"Have you ever been arrested? Are there any outstanding warrants I need to know about?"

She shook her head no emphatically to both questions.

"Don't lie to me. I can easily find out and lying to a federal agent is a felony itself."

"I'm not lying," she said with conviction.

Compton said she had been out clubbing earlier and two girls she knew invited her along to a party later at the home of a man they said was a player, guy named Rahall. They said he gave meth like candy. Compton explained she was a sometime user. Tanner figured her urges more frequent but let it go. Compton said her boyfriend had lost his job and gone to Denver and she decided to go to the party with her club friends. She knew only their first names. When she got to his house Rahall latched onto her. She said he seemed agitated and talked almost non-stop. They were watching X-rated videos that Compton said she found boring. Then, she said, Rahall got up and left the room for a few minutes and the others headed for the bedrooms.

"We were all using Meth, crack, and drinking. There were five of us besides Tomas. And the others, my friends and two men who said they worked with Rahall, went into the bedroom." She looked down at the floor, her face flushed. "I don't do sex that casual and didn't want that group action."

Tanner nodded, "Yeah?"

Compton said she thought of leaving but then thought she'd take a little more meth, and then Rahall came back in the room with a big pistol. That froze her in place.

"He unloaded it. Then he put one bullet back in it. He spun the thing where bullets go, put the barrel to his head and pulled the trigger. Nothing happened. I nearly fainted but he only laughed. I wanted to get out of there and tried to get up but he grabbed my arm and held me back. Then he put another bullet in it and spun the cylinder and pulled the trigger again. When the gun did not fire, he kept putting bullets in it until all the chambers were loaded."

"And no one tried to stop him?"

"Everybody else had gone in the bedroom. I was so scared but every time I tried to get up he'd reach out and hold me with one hand while he held the pistol with another. And I was afraid he would point it at me, that he'd shoot me if I struggled. I kept saying 'Please.'"

Compton began crying. Tanner looked around the office, saw a box of tissues on a desk and brought it to her. He excused himself for a moment and grabbed her can of Coke from the office refrigerator. She dabbed at her eyes and blew her nose and thanks him. When she calmed a little he said, "Go ahead."

"I was begging him to stop, but he laughed. Crazy. I wanted to get away from him. So help me…" She choked for a moment and let out a sob. "He put his pistol to his cheek, and he turned his head to me, and he said, "Bye." And he pulled the trigger. It was so loud I thought the trailer bounced. And I was there . . . I was covered with . . . stuff . . . all over me."

Compton's breathing was ragged and she was trembling. She tried to take a drink of Coke but had trouble putting it to her mouth.

Tanner put a hand on her shoulder. He gave her a few minutes to compose herself and said he wanted to test something.

"I want to walk through this. Just wait a minute. " He left the room and came back with a Ruger Blackhawk 44.magnum revolver like the one found on Rahall's trailer floor. Compton stiffened when she saw it. Tanner assured her the weapon was unloaded and even had a safety wire through the barrel.

"I'm going to be frank with you, Miss Compton. I don't see how a low to high shot could happen that way—not with a right handed man putting a pistol with a six-inch barrel into his left cheek." He got up and motioned her to do the same. "I want you to arrange the seating here just as it was in the trailer Friday night. Pretend these chairs are the sofa and then put me in the position Tomas was in before the shot. And you sit like you were sitting when it happened. "

"He was like this," she said turned Tanner so his body was angled toward her. "He held me with his left hand," and she put Tanner's on her right arm. "He turned his head a little away from me, to his right, as he cut his eyes left toward me," she said, and she put Tanner's right hand to his left cheek. "Bang," she said very softly.

That's it! Tanner saw it was the only position possible. It could happen if Rahall was perched on the edge of the couch just like that. As he ran it through his head again he looked at her purse sitting on the edge of his desk. It had some faint burgundy and gray flecks on one side, as if they had been sprayed there. Suddenly, he reached over and pointed to her purse and asked, "You had this with you? Where was it?"

"At my feet."

"Point to the floor where it was exactly," he instructed.

She did and he said, "I believe you. Look at your purse. See the discolored spots on your purse? It's from Rahall—blood and brain matter."

She gagged and edged away from the purse. "I'm feeling sick, I need the women's room," she said. He led her to it and waited outside.

"I'll need your purse," he told her when she came out. "Here's an evidence bag you can carry your stuff home. I suspect even after we're through analyzing the spots, you won't want it back."

"I don't. I already threw away my clothes from the other night. If I'd noticed this . . .

"Will you be all right?"

"I'm okay. I'm not sleeping much and I can't forget what happened. I just didn't want some innocent person to be arrested. I got your name from, uh, someone I went out with once. He's a, a former cop, Earl Bowman? I told him I was afraid of local police and he said you'd hear me out."

"You did the right thing coming forward," Tanner said. "You're still going to have to go through this again with the Fountain police. I'll take you down there and talk you through it;"

He got her another Coke and went to his desk to call LaForce.

"Rahall was suicide," he told the detective."

"Bullshit."

"Nope. Real deal. Got you an eyewitness. She walked in with splatter evidence, showed me how it happened. Give us an hour and I'll bring her down. She'll convince you."

"Only thing I'm convinced of now is how impossibly weird that whole scene really was. That Rahall would'a fucked up a two-car funeral."

Early the next morning Tanner called Tirado and said it was time to be introduced as a buyer of meth who could have some interesting weapons to sell from time to time.

"I'll be Sam. From Kansas," he said. "You'll say I deal in meth and guns while I operate a small taxi company."

"That could work."

"Oh it'll work. I'll be down to get you in my cab about noon. Call Ramon Pacheco and tell him you'll be bringing me by."

The taxi was a six-year-old Taurus with 180,000 miles that ATF dumped from the fleet. It had been sent to a Kansas City cab company, painted and kitted out as a regular taxi, with a light dome on the roof that housed a video camera with dash controls and a meter that housed another video camera focused on the vehicle interior, which was wired for sound. The camera and a tape recorder could be activated by the driver pressing a knee to a switch. So far the agency had used the fake taxi only for loose surveillance, but it seemed perfect for what Tanner had in mind.

When he picked up Tirado at Piazza's Pizza, he searched the informant to make sure he wasn't carrying a weapon into the meeting and then began wiring him with a transmitter.

"Hold still. Don't be so hinkey, I've got your back. This is a simple fucking buy and all you have to do is keep cool. Just call Pacheco and tell him your car is dead and a friend who's a cabby has agreed to drive you."

Tanner wanted his first exposure to Pacheco to be brief, even if only a hello. He could see that Tirado was too frightened for the insider role and realized he would have to ease Tirado out of the picture quickly. He decided to wear his own wire also in case he was invited into the house and couldn't decline without raising suspicion.

For this meeting he gave Tirado $3,600 to buy a quarter pound of crystal. When they got to the cab, Tirado started to open the back door.

"Get in front," Tanner ordered.

"Wouldn't a passenger ride in the back?"

"Look, numb nuts. I'm supposed to be your buddy, not a regular cab driver you called. Friends don't chauffer each other around with one riding in back."

Ten minutes later as they approached Pacheco's house, Tirado suddenly said, "Stop the car. There he is."

Tirado pointed to a Hispanic man sitting on the curb a block from his own address. He stood up, a slender man in his late twenties with a wispy mustache, and walked over to the cab.

"Hey, amigo," Pacheco said.

"Ramon, this is an old friend, Sam. Agreed to give me a lift. Don't know what the fuck's wrong with my car but didn't have time to find out. Why are you out here?"

"Just having a smoke and looking around the neighborhood on a nice afternoon. I'll meet you at the house."

As they pulled ahead and Pacheco followed on foot, Tirado said, "Nice day my ass. This guy trusts nobody. He out to make certain nobody's closing in on him and he isn't being set up. He doesn't like making direct sales, leaves that up to the distributors, but I convinced him this was a start of something big."

Tirado climbed out of the car at Pacheco's address and waited on the porch for him. Tanner wasn't invited inside with them and stayed in the cab, listening in on the receiver while the buy went down. Afterward they rode back to the ATF office where Tirado was debriefed and unwired and the drugs and the tape of the buy locked in the evidence room.

"Okay, you did well," Tanner said. "I've got to go out of town on assignment for a few days, and you need to keep out of trouble.
"All you have to do is keep out of trouble while I'm gone. That means you don't get into any active deals. Just keep your ear to the ground, line up some action for next week and we'll run hard then."

Tirado promised, but Tanner thought his pledge to keep his hands clean was a little too glib. It must have showed.

"You can trust me, Sam," the informant urged.

"Understand something, Richard. You can trust me to watch your back. But trust between us is a one-way street. And it's short."

9

September is when Federal agencies begin looking for ways to spend everything left in their yearly budget so when they ask for an increase the next year – and it's the rule to always ask for more money -- the bean counters can't accuse them of not needing what they already got. ATF's western region chief decided the best way to spend some surplus was to employ a Special Response Team to help bring down a meth cooker in the Missouri Ozarks said to be heavily protected. Tanner was a sniper on the regional team, and an SRT assignment generally took precedence on an agent's agenda.

Tanner would leave for Missouri tomorrow, so with his undercover job on hold he was doing what a dedicated federal agent does in slow circumstances, catching up on the never ending mountain of paperwork, when Josh Groton walked into his office and took the best chair.

"What do you have on for this afternoon?" he asked. "Got a meeting I want you to take, with Ed Dennison and it's about your case."

Tanner couldn't help but bristle. "What the hell does the FBI know about my case?"

"Well, it turns out that…"

"That they want to take it over," Tanner finished Groton's sentence for him.

"Not exactly," Groton said. "You know Ed's a good guy. He's one of the few Freebies we can get along with."

Ed Dennison was a former ATF agent who had worked the hard streets of Camden, New Jersey in the Eighties, until his partner was killed during a bust. Dennison was so shaken he decided to get out of gun work and went to night law school. He took a job as an assistant

U.S. attorney but ultimately missed the street life and signed on with the FBI. Tanner believed that his heart was still with ATF even if his head was somewhere else. If the FBI insisted on butting into this operation, Tanner knew Dennison would be fair.

"We decided that maybe you and I and Ed and his case agent would meet and see if there wasn't some mutual ground for cooperation, maybe a joint operation. Groton said. "He said their man has been keeping an eye on this for several months."

"Okay," Tanner said. "But I'll tell you what, Josh. Any cooperation, even with Ed keeping an eye on things, is always going to be one way, the FBI's."

The meeting took place in mid-afternoon in the ATF conference room. Tanner had been instructed to bring his entire case file. When he walked into the room, he found Groton and Dennison sitting at either end of the table and an unsmiling agent named Ben Short, sitting between. Tanner had been briefed about Short, a former Army captain who was the youngest FBI agent in Colorado Springs and said to be prickly. Or as Tanner's source said, "Drop the l and y, he's just a prick."

With no more than a nod at introductions, Short informed Tanner he was aware of his working on FBI targets and that he should give up his files. Tanner could feel his face redden but said evenly, "I'll tell you what Agent Short, why don't we each outline what we have and let our bosses decide who should keep going."

Short talked for twenty minutes about collecting information on the Pacheco organization for the past year, now and then tapping a thick file on the table he said contained reports on significant details. When he was done, Tanner said, "I want to make sure I understand. Your team has spent eighteen months tracking and collecting intelligence on this outfit and you have a complete and full file right there to back it up. That right?"

"Correct," said Short.

"And to date you have not made one buy or executed one search warrant?

Short bristled. "That's correct."

Tanner noted he'd been on the case for less than two months, pausing while Short looked over to smile at Dennison. Then Tanner explained he had a confidential informant inside the organization, had personally witnessed several buys of drugs and handguns from several targets and had successfully inserted an undercover agent into the heart of a multi-state operation. He did not identify himself as the one undercover but said he had evidence including guns and drugs locked up in the ATF vault.

"So while it has taken you eighteen months to go nowhere, in a couple of months I have gone to the point I could arrest several high-ups in the organization and be prepared to testify at trial tomorrow. So why don't you work with me?"

Groton agreed, proposing that Sam be the lead since he had the informant and the undercover operative, and Dennison agreed. To their surprise Short stood up, pushed his folder across the table and said to his startled boss, "He wants it, he can have it. But I will not work a case jointly if Tanner or anyone else in ATF is the lead. I'm out of it," He stalked out of the room.

Dennison flushed with embarrassment and stood up, shaking hands with Tanner and apologizing for his agent's behavior.

"I'll work with your guy if things change," Tanner said.

The FBI supervisor turned around at the door and said, "No you don't want to be doing that." He paused and added, "After today's performance, Agent Short will be chasing stolen property from Ft. Carson for as long as he's assigned under me."

The SRT assignment had a good outcome for everyone but the Missouri meth cooker, one Bobby Joe Alley. Bringing agents from all over the West used up heaps of government dollars that might not have gotten otherwise wasted, so the supervisors were happy. And Tanner didn't have to shoot anybody. In fact he was stationed a hundred yards out from Alley's rambler in the hollow, and there were so many agents swarming the scene that Tanner barely got a look at the bad guy when he was led out in handcuffs. The only downside to the raid that anybody noticed was every officer who'd crept through the woods got chewed by chiggers, and Tanner scratched furtively at his three bites in rude places the whole flight home.

He was fresh from the shower and giving Sally, dressed fetchingly in nothing, a look of particular significance when the bedside phone rang. He figured to let it go unanswered but couldn't resist looking at the caller ID and seeing Fountain Police on the screen.

"Uh-oh, Babe, gotta take it."

"Sam, Jim Sanderson in Fountain. I have a minor problem here."

"None of your problems are ever minor," Tanner countered. "Who got killed this time?"

The Fountain chief explained that two of his patrolmen had responded to a suspicious vehicle call earlier in the evening. Inside the car were a woman and a man they recognized as Richard Tirado, who had been picked up in Fountain previously with guns and passports and dope. The woman in the driver's seat identified herself as Tammy Chisholm from Colorado Springs.

The officers asked Tirado's permission to search the 2005 Tahoe and he responded it wasn't his and he wasn't driving. They then asked Chisholm and she said the car was Tirado's. They asked her to step out of the vehicle and when she did they noticed a pistol on the floor of the driver's side. In a custodial search they discovered a fully loaded Walther PPK .380 caliber pistol and a pound of substance they field-tested and identified as methamphetamine along with almost $1,000 in cash."

"Tirado told the arresting officer when he was out of Chisholm's presence and she couldn't hear him that he was working for an ATF agent as a confidential informant. He claimed the agent knew all about what he was doing. When questioned further he named you as the agent."

Tanner's jaw clenched. "He mentioned me directly?"

"Yeah, he did. Both to the officer and when the officer contacted me, I came on in and he repeated it to me. If that's the case, Sam, I can make this go away."

Tanner was furious but not surprised. He'd anticipated some fuck-up by Tirado but this put his undercover op at risk. His policy on informants was firm. If one committed a crime while working for him, that ended the arrangement.

"Jim I appreciate this, particularly since you came in at this late hour but I warned this dumb son of a bitch, who is supposed to have this big time IQ, from the minute he's caught with drugs or a weapon he is not working for me. Can you get him in your office and put him on the speaker phone?"

A few minutes later Tanner heard Sanderson telling Tirado to have a seat. "Okay," the chief said, "You're on the speaker phone."

"Hello, Chief Sanderson, how are you?" Tanner said.

"Fine," the chief responded, going with the charade.

"What do you have for me?" Tanner said.

"I have Richard C. Tirado here in my office."

"Who?"

"Richard Cameron Tirado."

"I never heard of him," Tanner said. "I don't know him and whatever he is claiming regarding my association with him and his activities this evening is false. My advice to you Chief Sanderson is to charge him, book him in the county jail and I will take these and the other charges federally when I return at the end of the week. Thank you for your call."

"Very well and thank you for your time, agent Tanner," Sanderson said and hung up.

Fifteen minutes later Tanner redialed Sanderson and asked how Tirado had taken it.

"Not well," the chief said. "He turned white as a sheet. I thought he was going to collapse."

"Good. Now tell me about the girl. Are you holding her?"

"My guys have her in interrogation now. But Tirado said she had no knowledge of what was going on, that they had just been on a date."

"Right," Tanner said. "That's crap and you know it. But I don't want her nailed on this now. We already have enough evidence to arrest her but she's likely small potatoes. I think you could cut her loose."

After hanging up Tanner lay back in bed and stared at the ceiling considering his dilemma. While he hated to lose the informant, his usefulness was almost gone with the latest arrest. The Pachecos wouldn't trust him when he kept getting caught. They'd know if he suddenly reappeared on the street after another bust it had to be because he was talking to cops. This might give Tanner a chance to insert himself directly into the Pacheco's business, though.

Sally poked him in the ribs and he turned to see that while he'd been busy on the phone she had slipped into some unrevealing.

"Aw," he said.

"I think you're more in the mood to talk," she said.

"No, I think you are."

"Well let's try talking and see who wants to move to something else first."

When he said nothing she said, "What I can't understand is if the Pacheco's are as big an operation as you think they are, why every one of them you come in contact with are such complete fuckups."

Tanner considered that a minute. "Keep in mind I haven't gotten to the top operators. Ramon and Maria and whoever else they might be getting supplies from could well be very different. It looks like they've been operating under the radar here for a long time and that suggests they're smart and careful."

"Okay," she conceded. "But you tell me you've gone to a homicide scene where supplies for making meth are kept in a safe but money is left sitting around in boxes. And a guy put in charge of where they're doing their business is having orgies and playing Russian roulette on the premises. I just can't see any logic."

Tanner couldn't help his laugh. "Sweetie, if we looked for logic we'd never catch them. We anticipate the illogical. These people, they're not wired like us. They put drugs in a safe and leave money lying around because to them the meth is what's valuable. The money is something they probably owe to somebody else. Really. They just don't think like ordinary people. These are people who ingest industrial cleaning solvents. It's what meth is. What happens is that any drug operation is bound to be always unraveling somewhere at the edges, where it's user unfriendly, and the bosses are always going patch, patch, patch."

He saw in the corner of his eye that Sally was shrugging out of her nightie. She'd played him like a puppet, getting him talking and drawing him out of his funk. The night wasn't young but there was time to get in touch with their inner adolescents.

And the phone rang.

Sally leaned across him to intercept it, saw who it was on caller ID and knew the call this late couldn't be ignored. She couldn't help but say it, "If it isn't one thing, it's your mother."

10

Maria Pacheco didn't believe Tirado could afford a bond again even with a rich aunt. She knew he'd squeal to get a shorter sentence and the person he'd give up first would be her son

"Handle it," she said.

Manny Suarez took a last drag on his cigarette, snubbed it out on an ashtray on her desk and nodded. "It will cost $20,000."

"How does it happen?"

"I know a man waiting extradition to Mexico. He has a wife and two kids here. He will do it for assurance his family will be taken care of until his troubles are over."

Maria went to her safe and took out four banded stacks of bills.

Manny was at the El Paso County Jail when afternoon visiting hours began at four. He showed the desk sergeant a driver's license that identified him as Rafael Gallegos of Denver. He had no mustache and the photo on the license did but the officer only glanced at it, more concerned with the change in his pockets that made the metal detector light up. Manny said he wished to see his cousin Jose Contraras and was buzzed through to an anteroom where he sat down at a table and waited.

"*Esto es una mierda*," he said when Contraras took a seat across the table from him. Contraras solemnly agreed this was shit.

"I worry for your wife and children," Manny told him.

"I too, *patron*. I don't know what I do."

Manny explained in low tones he had a solution. He said he had concerns about a man in the jail named Richard Tirado and described

him carefully down to a mole on his upper lip and the USMC tattooed
on the inside of his right forearm

"I know that one," Contreras said.

"You understand what I need?" Manny asked, and Contreras gave
a nod.

Manny said he would make a $10,000 down payment to Contreras's
family in Fountain that very day and that he would make a similar gift
when it was done, if that was satisfactory.

When he got word from his wife that a man had left her the money
he would do it, Contreras said. "I always call her after dinner and she
will tell me then." He called her at 8 p.m.

Richard Tirado didn't get a bite of breakfast. The bell for it sounded
and he was standing with a dozen others in the hallway at the door to
the mess hall when a voice behind his right shoulder said, "Hey Tick-
Tock, something here for you." He turned unthinking toward it and a
sharpened tang of a serving spoon slid under his sternum and upward,
and back and forth.

Jose Contreras let go of the spoon's bowl wrapped in his handkerchief,
left it sticking there, and turned and walked away.

Tirado's jaw opened but he said nothing, looked down at the spoon
in his heart and the hanky falling to the floor now and the blood
just welling where it punctured him, his eyes wide in shock-pain-fear-
disbelief. As his knees buckled he got out, "ohhhhh," then, "shi-i-i,"
but not loudly at all and the inmates were looking down at him more
in curiosity than alarm. Then they noticed the spoon and involuntarily
stepped back, every one. Somebody said "Jesus" but no one bent to help.
Tirado's mouth moved but no words came, and then his brown eyes,
that had looked up at the men in hurt but not focused on any one, saw
nothing.

The inmates looked at him, looked quickly at each other, then
stared at him hardly comprehending. They stepped further back when
his bowels let go. "Whooey," said somebody. Then they were looking
all around. This stuff never happened in county lockup.

Jose Contreras wasn't there to be seen. He'd gone back to his cell. He
wasn't required to eat breakfast. He'd be impatient for lunch, though.
This thing that he'd done before, when it didn't make you sick it built
all kinds of appetites.

He lay on his bunk while the whistles blew and the deputies started running.

Every inmate was questioned. Nobody saw nothin', each said. No arrest was imminent. Inquiries continued, as the sheriff's news release stated. Or as he said privately, "Along the line of what the fuck?"

ATF had no clues either.

Josh Gorton tried to get Tanner to shrug off his guilt about Tirado's murder. "I know you must feel bad about this, Sam, but your actions were correct. Who'd figure the Pachecos would react like that?"

"I should have," Tanner replied. "I had a feeling they wouldn't trust him in and out a second time. But, and I may be rationalizing here, if I'd made the arrest go away they would have smelled a rat and the result could have been the same. I just had no idea they would have anybody in county lockup who could pull this off, not so quick like that."

Groton shook his head. "There must be a couple dozen illegals in the El Paso County jail right now. And who knows the first thing about their priors? They're questioning all of 'em but chances of getting anything are fucking nada. There's no leverage. Every one's waiting extradition or being deported as I speak."

One point they agreed on was Tanner should move into the vacuum left by Tirado and take advantage of his introduction to Ramon Pacheco. And Groton laid out a plan to accomplish it based on the meth deal that Tanner wired and taped while he waited outside Pacheco's house. First ATF filed for a sealed search warrant, to protect Tanner's identity until Pacheco was actually arrested. The next step called for some street theater by the agents, who would execute the warrant. They'd pretend to find a technical error in the paperwork that rendered the search unlawful, even though they'd say it did allow them to collect weapons, drugs and money. They'd claim it meant they couldn't arrest Pacheco for possession.

To protect his undercover identity Tanner took a leave day to go fishing while Groton led a team of federal and local officers in the raid.

It was 4 a.m. when they began pounding on Pacheco's door and 4:05 before a women opened it. She wore a blank expression and a

Bronco's t-shirt that reached to her knees and apparently nothing else. When told they were here to search the premises, she ran to the back of the house calling, "Ramon."

The officers took that as invitation to enter and followed, rounding up Ramon and herself in one bedroom and another man and woman in a second. They were handcuffed, led to the kitchen and made to sit on the floor. The team quickly found two pounds of meth so fresh it looked like it had been cooked that day, along with twenty rifles, pistols and shotguns and enough drug paraphernalia to fill a large cardboard box.

Groton was reading their rights to Pacheco and his guests, when DEA Agent Mike Reach walked into the room holding the search warrant, showed it to Groton and said loudly enough for all to hear, "Sir, you'd better check this out. I just noticed it's missing the signature."

"What?" Groton exclaimed, snatching it out of Reach's hands. "I don't believe it."

"Sorry, Sir," Reach muttered, looking down at the floor as if ashamed. "I don't know how that got by me."

Groton stomped around the kitchen, opening and slamming cabinets and kicking the waste can. He shook a meaty finger in Reach's face, "Agent, your fuckup means they can't be arrested. They're all going to walk because of this. Hope you're going to like your next assignment, freezing your balls off in Nome."

Pacheco stared up at the officers, trying to keep a smile from his face, and holding his hands out to them. "You going to take these cuffs off?"

In pretended chagrin the officers did that, checked the IDs and made notes of addresses, then began hauling out the guns and drugs.

"We're still taking this as evidence," Groton said angrily. Then he leaned into Pacheco's face, "You can come down to the station and claim it as yours, of course. Then we *can* arrest you."

All Pacheco said to that was, "Bye officers."

Tanner spent all of Thursday waist deep in the South Platt, getting a sun-scorched nose, a sore right shoulder, a deerfly bite on his neck and landing one golden trout six inches long. By the time he got to the office next morning his catch had grown to three trout none less than twelve inches. It didn't matter, nobody wanted to hear about it.

"The best place for the skilled angler yesterday was Ramon Pacheco's House," Groton boasted. "While you were matching wits with a creature of no IQ and likely losing, I was confounding a master criminal. You should have seen me reel in the lunker."

Mike Reach had come down from the DEA office on the floor above and lifted his mug of coffee to toast Groton. "You should have heard him lay it down," he told Tanner. "If bullshit were asphalt Josh Groton would be Route 66."

Groton laughed, "We follow the letter of the law here, but there's no law that says we can't mess with their heads. Pacheco really thinks he skated because the warrant wasn't signed, even though I showed him the paper with the magistrate's signature on it plain as the stupid look on his face."

"The devil's in the details," Tanner sagely offered.

"Indeed she is," said Groton.

For the next hour the three concocted how Tanner could happen to bump into Pacheco in a believable way. The plan called for asking Pacheco's probation officer to summon him for a meeting to talk about associating with known criminals, since both women found at his home had busts on record for prostitution. Tanner would be there in his rigged taxi and intercept Pacheco when he left the building.

The morning of the meeting Tanner loaded the cab's video with fresh tape and ran a check on all electrical connections. He put a duffle bag holding two handguns and an automatic rifle on the passenger side floor of the front seat and drove to the county courthouse followed by Groton and Reach in separate cars. Spotting an empty space three cars away from Pacheco's Tahoe, Tanner pulled the cab into it, got out of the cab and sat on the trunk facing the building's ornate brass double doors. He took his cell phone out of his pocket, dialed the probation office and said, "I'm in place, you can cut him loose."

Groton and Reach, each parked in a blocking position, flashed their lights to signal they could hear Tanner on his wire.

Tanner's head was down, looking at his cell phone when the little drug boss walked past on the way to his car. Tanner glanced up as if surprised and said, "Hey."

The young man turned and stared at him warily.

"Remember me?" said Tanner.

11

Ramon Pacheco stopped and looked Tanner up and down. He gave no sign of recognition. Tanner pretended Pacheco wasn't pretending.

"I'm Sam, Richard Tirado's friend. I drove him to your place the other day."

Pacheco stood there unsmiling. "I remember. You look like a cop."

Tanner burst out laughing. He was ready for this one because he saw himself in the mirror every morning: a big man, no giant but a bit over six feet, thirty pounds, okay forty, past 200, thick shoulders, thick waist, thick wrists, big nose, big chin, big feet. Everything about him large and hard except his eyes, small and hard, and his lips, thin and hard. "You're under arrest," he joked, laughing on until a smile started to form unbidden on Pacheco's own un-cop-like face. "Can't tell you how often this," Tanner said, pointing a thick finger at his wide mug, "has gotten me out of tight spots. Cops look me over and they think I 'm one of 'em, on the side of law and order anyway, drive right on by." Which was of course the truth.

Pacheco was grinning openly now. "What you want?"

"I've been out of town on a collection matter. I've been trying to reach Richard about some product and can't find him anywhere."

"How long you been gone?"

"Week."

"Well he got arrested and then somebody killed him in lockup." Pacheco was measuring Tanner's reaction.

"Whoa. That's terrible!" Tanner stood up. "I can't believe it. Who did it?"

Pacheco shrugged.

"How'd it go down?"

"Somebody stick him."

"Ah." Tanner winced. "I'm real sorry about that." He waited a beat and added, "But hey you were his partner. Richard and I had some business going and maybe you'd want to pick up his end."

"Yeah?"

Tanner glanced around the lot. "Let's don't go into it out here. How about hopping into my cab here and we can drive around."

Pacheco hesitated a moment. "Can't be too long. I got business." When he got in the front seat he had to get his feet around the big bag on the floorboard.

"A delivery I'm making tonight," Tanner explained. "Taking it to Topeka. Have a look for yourself."

As Tanner pulled out of the lot, turning right to make a wide looping drive around the courthouse, Pacheco bent down and unbuckled the bag, lifting out an Ingram Mac 10 with a silencer. The wariness he'd shown getting into the car fell away and he grinned. "Damn. Nice. Where you get that? Nobody here got a piece like that." He hefted the weapon and tried the bolt."

"Check out the other stuff," Tanner said, heading for the Interstate. "I'll just ride us out to Castle Rock and back, okay?"

Pacheco grunted approval as he dug into the bag and fished out a new in the box Browning BDM 9mm and then a holstered Smith & Wesson .357 XVR magnum. He was laughing now. "What's one of these cost me?" he demanded.

"Sorry," Tanner said, "these aren't for sale. Got a buyer for them. I might be able to do you right on something else, though."

ATF could not put weapons on the street. Undercover agents could buy illegal guns to build a case against the seller but could never be the source for a gun that could be used in a crime. Tanner would string a buyer along but never deliver weapons or drugs. He'd buy and buy, until there was a strong case to raid and confiscate more guns and the money he'd spent buying. The story he began to lay out now was to show he was more than a second tier thug like his old Army pal Tirado. His plan was to be seen as a significant player who could bring the Pacheco's new sources of revenue.

"I buy guns of all types. I get them here and I haul them out of state, sell 'em in Kansas City, Oklahoma City, places far from where I buy them. So they don't come back to bite me."

"Got that," Pacheco said, "Mind if I smoke."

"Yeah, hold off. I don't want cigarette smell in the taxi. I use it as a legitimate front." He stopped at a light on Arapaho.

"Look," Tanner said, "I can maybe find you a special piece, as a favor you understand. But my business flows the other way. I've had some customers wanting dope, and I was talking with Tirado about supplying some of that action. And he was supposed to be getting me some guns. I've got sources but I thought I'd see what he could do."

A woman in a blue Beemer cut in front of the cab and Tanner tapped the horn. She flipped him the bird as she drew away, him thinking, *Lady, if you only had a clue.* He pulled into a strip mall lot so he could stop and look Pacheco in the eye while he sent a message.

"The dope Tirado got from you when I drove him there was really for me, and I've moved it. Fact of the matter, I can move all the dope and guns I can get but finding a steady supplier is a problem. I thought I had something worked out with Richard and now he's dead. I'm thinking you and I could put something together."

Pacheco was stretched back in the seat, hands locked behind his head, relaxed now and liking the way this was going. "Well, I could have had a real good deal for you," he said. "A few days ago I had a stash of meth I could have let go, but ATF raided my house and took everything."

"Why aren't you in jail then?" Tanner asked.

Pacheco gave a snort. "You wouldn't believe. They fucked up, didn't get the warrant signed. The guy who did it got his ass chewed right in front of me. They could confiscate my stuff but couldn't arrest me for having it. How about that? Only thing, I've lost my inventory at the moment, couple dozen guns and two pounds of meth."

"So what are you doing here," Tanner asked as if suddenly suspicious. "Talking to anybody?"

"No man. Just seeing my PO about something old, it was a first offense and probation."

A squad car pulled into the lot and rolled past them, the officer giving them a casual look-over and Pacheco going wary. Tanner waited until the patrolman was well past them, then started up and drove toward I-25.

Pacheco settled and said, "I'll have a resupply of meth in a couple days. But if you want some guns I can put hands on 'em pretty quick."

"Any sawed-offs?"

Pacheco said he could get two that afternoon. They agreed on a hundred dollars for each and arranged to meet after lunch at a Fountain park with a fishing pond located just off the Interstate. When Tanner arrived he found Pacheco sitting atop a picnic table and watching a brindle pit bull take a dump.

A middle-aged woman with white standard poodle on a leash stood about fifty feet away glaring at the scene. When the pit bull finished and Pacheco made no move to clean up after him, the woman shouted at him, "Pick it up."

Pacheco waved her away.

"Pick it up," she shouted again.

Pacheco turned and called out, "Lady, I don't really want it. I don't have any use for it. But you can have it."

It enraged her. She shouted, "Pick it up, pick it up," practically stamping her foot.

Tanner couldn't believe a woman in control of her faculties would challenge strangers in an empty park this way and he hoped he wouldn't have to step out of role to save her dumb ass.

Pacheco was happy to goose her to apoplexy, calling, "Come get it. It would look good on you."

She quivered at the insult, made as if to come closer, then seemed to take in at last the now-rigid pit bull, the grinning hard-eyed Hispanic man, and the big white guy with the gunfighter mustache, all of them staring at her, and she turned abruptly and pulled her poodle close and huffed away.

It made Pacheco laugh, "See how it is? People all the time trying to give you shit."

Tanner wanted to laugh too now the absurd scene was defused but kept his face straight. "And we'd be in the shit if she finds a cop. Lets do the business and split."

Pacheco put his dog in his car and brought the shotguns wrapped in a blanket to the cab. The deal was done with the video rolling.

Everybody back at the ATF viewing it later agreed Ramon Pacheco looked handsome on camera, a Latino Brad Pitt, but they wished he'd articulate just a little more clearly.

"Tries to be cool, that lazy way of talking," said Groton. "But you know, I think the kid's got a future in film." It cracked them up.

There was just one scene played again and again in the movie ATF was making. Because of the raid on Ramon' house Tanner said he didn't want to trade in drugs and guns there or anyplace where the dealer had operated before. And Tanner emphasized that he had never been arrested himself, was not a user but was in fact a careful and successful businessman.

"But you seem to be on their radar now," Tanner said. "Trust me, the cab is the safest place we can do business."

It was important to record Pacheco making buy after buy in the taxi because each would be a separate count in the ultimate indictment and all together would be evidence of a criminal conspiracy. In their second meeting Tanner bought two ounces of meth. In their third he bought two more ounces and an M-16 stolen from an area military base. As important to the investigation as each deal was the conversation, which became easier with every meeting. A friendship of a sort was growing as Ramon discovered Sam from Kansas to be a dependable source of income and a good listener, too. They could really talk. With his top two lieutenants dead, Ramon had no one else of comparable stature he could chew over troubles with, and there was something about the big man behind the wheel that invited confidence. Ramon was beginning to think here was somebody to bring in to back him up, and he was about ready to take it up with his mother. She was wary of strange Anglos but Sam, he was different, she'd see that.

Ramon had brought her up in their first meeting. He said the raid cost his outfit probably twenty grand in street profits and "My mother ripped the hide off me."

Tanner played incredulous, "Your mother knows about all this?"

"You don't know who my mother is?" Ramon asked.

"Should I?"

Ramon shook his head and changed the subject, apparently reconsidering what he'd been about to say. He mentioned her again in their second meeting but got vague when Tanner showed interest. It was a month after their first ride and they were parked on the grounds of the Broadmoor Hotel, eating takeout burritos and eyeing two power-walking hotties in shorts, when Tanner proposed making a bulk purchase of meth and Ramon said, "I'll ask my mom."

It occurred to Tanner he'd never heard a grown man say that, but showed no wonder as he asked Ramon to explain. With the video rolling, Ramon did.

Ramon said that when he was ten his stepfather died of a heart attack, leaving his mother with three young children and a small insurance policy. Maria needed work right away and her great luck was to have a niece working as a clerk at Clemons Health Supplements. She interviewed for work there but only to scope it out from the inside. From her niece she was aware of a far richer opportunity than a job from nine to five. Clemons was illegally using large quantities of ephedrine and, as Maria knew very well, it's the main ingredient in methamphetamine.

Clemons, which produced vitamins and herbal remedies, had relocated to Colorado a few years before from Texas after the deaths of several college students using its diet aids. The company was sued and assessed damages and ordered to cease and desist, and the Food and Drug Administration put the firm on a watch. After moving and changing its name, the executives couldn't resist the money to be made hawking its ephedrine pills. It found a source in China and began paying cash for it there, keeping under the FDA's radar. From her niece Maria learned there were no records being kept by Clemons for the ephedrine being shipped in fifty-five pound cardboard barrels and stored in an off-site warehouse several miles from the main manufacturing facility near Fountain. Her niece, who agreed to let Maria know whenever supplies arrived, passed her a key to the warehouse. Maria checked for herself, and as her niece said security at the warehouse was nonexistent. Maria Pacheco, then thirty-five, a petite and attractive mother of four living in a one-bedroom house in a shabby suburb and driving a ten-year-old car, literally held in her hands the key to a narco empire.

Tanner was stunned on two levels, that such an operation could flourish here where law enforcement was concentrated and that Ramon was actually laying out so much the operation out for him.

"This is incredible," Tanner told him. "What a set up. Your mother is some kind of genius. How long has this been going on?"

"Fifteen years." Ramon laughed, taking in Tanner's genuine amazement.

"Man, she's got the meth business by the balls."

Ramon quit laughing. "Yeah, she did until she went back to California three years ago. She went by herself to deliver ephedrine to a major cooker in the desert and to pick up some finished product."

"So what happened?" Tanner asked when he paused.

Pacheco explained that after making her delivery Maria stopped at a burger place and was shot during a failed car-jacking attempt. After she was rushed to a hospital, police found several ounces of meth under the front seat of her car in a routine search.

Maria had never been exposed before and now she was in a predicament facing the likelihood of lengthy court proceedings. And bossing her organization required constant presence and attention.

"She discussed it with me in her hospital room," Ramon said, almost embarrassed. "She wanted me to fill the leadership vacuum but said I wasn't ready. I had to say she was right. But she had to do something. Then we made a mistake."

A football sailed from somewhere on the Broadmoor's lawn and whanged on the hood of the taxi, making them both jump. They laughed, and Ramon opened his door saying he had to go find a bush to pee behind. He picked up the ball and lofted it back to a boy standing thirty yards away with his arms raised. While he was out, Tanner took the opportunity to hit the sound toggle twice, and from his left came a beep-beep he took as a signal from one of his backups that the conversation was coming through clearly.

Listening to the young man spill his family's secrets, Tanner had found himself in a curious sort of sympathy with Maria Pacheco. She had built something truly remarkable with her own wits, but she was right about her son. He wasn't ready to succeed her then or now and he never would be. He was bringing them down.

Tanner figured this was a good time to ask about the killing of Tirado. He knew it would back Ramon off if he was involved himself, but it would be a coup if a murder charge could be proved on someone in the organization. When Ramon got back from taking his leak Tanner said as if the thought just came, "Hey, I've been sitting here wondering, what happened with my friend Richard? Who'd he piss off?"

Ramon answered without hesitation, "I wish I knew. There was so much in Richard's background. He owed people. I just don't know."

Tanner could believe it. Ramon' puzzlement looked real and if Maria had ordered the hit she probably would not have told her son. She'd have had his lifetime to understand what Tanner had realized in a handful of meetings, Ramon' mouth ran a marathon. In a crisis she wouldn't count on him.

"You were saying something about a mistake," Tanner said.

Ramon frowned, locked fingers and popped his knuckles. He looked out the window as if seeing something distant, "Yeah, family, that's the mistake. It's Shorty, he fucked us."

As Ramon recalled it, he had come home from the hospital and was talking with his wife about how to keep the business going and her father who was visiting offered to help. Ramon' father-in-law Erineo Martinez, called Shorty, ran a small trucking company with his two brothers out of Monterey, Mexico. The Martinez's had started from scratch and were hard men in a hard business, and Ramon thought they had the experience and toughness to help him keep going. He took Shorty to see his mother the next morning.

Shorty suggested that Maria let him take over while she was recuperating. That is what a family does when one of its members is in need, he told her. He'd also be willing to keep providing assistance, if she wanted it, once she'd come back to resume command. And he pointed out that she could use his trucking business to expand her own when she was ready. Whatever suspicions Maria had, and Ramon at that point had none, they saw little choice but to let Erineo Martinez act as her surrogate while she got well and fought off her legal troubles in California.

"I see where this goes," said Tanner, understanding that Ramon was opening up to enlist ally in a struggle to take back the business from the Martinez brothers.

"Uh huh," Ramon agreed. "We'd been paying workers at Clemons $2,000 a barrel to turn their heads when we lifted the ephedrine. Right away he was paying them $10,000 a barrel and he bought their loyalty. Then he began charging the meth cooks $60,000 for every barrel he delivered them instead of the $10,000 that we'd demanded. Shorty had the muscle to enforce the price so they paid it."

Ramon said that Maria's cut kept getting squeezed to the point that lately she'd become little more than a figurehead in the manufacturing end but was allowed to keep running distributions through eastern Colorado and western Kansas. As a sweetener, the Martinez's had upped the amount that meth cooks sold back to Maria, from five to twenty-five pounds per load. But Ramon said that unless he could find a way to force his in-laws out, his mother was going to pack it in.

"She got millions, somewhere, man. But I got zip." Ramon said he was estranged now from his wife, and her family wasn't likely to leave him with much if his mother split.

Tanner stared out the windshield at nothing, tapping his fingers on the wheel as he mulled the implications. He'd been certain Maria Pacheco was pulling the strings but he saw her now as someone else's puppet. And he knew nothing about this Martinez family that was punking the Queen of Meth. He was being studied as he pondered.

Ramon suggested, "New friends could be useful."

Tanner agreed, "I could be useful." If Pacheco wanted muscle or money, he wanted to be called on for it. If a drug war were about to start the best place to head it off was from the inside. He gave Ramon a new cell phone number in case anything urgent came up.

"Maybe I can help," he said, not wanting to seem too eager. "People like that, something should be done."

12

When the video ended to whoops and applause, Josh Groton asked Tanner the questions that would be asked by any prosecutor taking the case to trial. "What did you do to this guy off-camera to get him to open up? Why would he lay all this out to a guy he'd met only a handful of times? Can we trust what he's saying?"

Tanner smiled and shrugged. He'd had to answer the same questions on other investigations. His record of drawing confessions from suspects had gotten him known around ATF as Father Sam. "As to what I did, nothing but ask and listen," he said, noting, "and we were under surveillance by my two backups the entire time we were together." As for why the subject talked so much, Tanner said, "The guns had a lot to do with it. He was overwhelmed by my hardware. He believes I'm somebody he can enlist to help him take down the Martinez brothers, and I think he's desperate to show his mother he's capable of climbing back on top."

Tanner said he would keep meeting with Ramon over the next several weeks to draw out more details -- about where the ephedrine is stashed after it's taken from the chemical company, and where it is moved from that point, and who are the mules.

Groton was giving Tanner a quizzical look. "I think you may have a few more things to do. You know about the Colorado Springs PD's supposed snitch?"

"Yeah?" The CPSD's secretive handling of a drug informant named Kennedy over several months had become something between a joke and a sore point at ATF. The locals had been reluctant to share anything coming from this source and the feds figured it was because they weren't getting anything of value. They had begun deriding the CPSD's source among themselves as Super Snitch.

"You been giving it much attention?"

Tanner hadn't and he had to admit it. "Not really."

"Well, their informant Kennedy keeps mentioning somebody named Shorty."

"Oh shit," said Tanner.

"You got it," said Groton.

Unless this was some amazing coincidence, which cops regard as likely as total honesty, there appeared to be two tracks into the Martinez/Pacheco organization and Tanner would have to follow both of them. Right away he'd have to contact CPSD about JoJo Kennedy, who he'd pretty much written off as a middle-aged poseur, to confirm whether his boss Shorty was the same as Erineo Martinez, the mystery man behind the Pachecos. And he had to be. That two Shorties controlled meth gangs in The Springs was as likely as there being another fed named Sam driving hoods around in a wired cab.

Tanner would scratch backs and twist arms at CPSD to get linked with their source, while Groton applied for wiretaps on executives of Clemons Health Supplements to build the case for a separate prosecution of the overseas purchases of ephedrine.

"I'm no spy."

Officer Taylor Rush sounded genuinely indignant at Tanner's request for some straight poop about what JoJo Kennedy was telling CPSD.

"Not asking you to spy on your department, Taylor. I'm requesting you to share a little information with your own government. And lets be straight. We both know you were assigned as liaison to ATF to report back on what we're doing, and I haven't squawked. Time for some quid pro, y'know? If I raised a stink about CPSD's non-cooperation in what's shaping up as a major guns and drugs op, there'd be hell to pay."

Rush stared unhappily at the hamburger he'd ordered, swigged his coke and nodded.

"I know, Sam. It's just Chief Beetle, he's paranoid about anybody from the outside operating on our turf."

"Hey, somebody needs to tell the chief, it's our turf, it's the United States."

Rush gave a small laugh, "Yeah. But the chief, you know, he's serially stupid."

"Now that, officer, is disloyal."

Rush laughed a little more, "Aw, fuck him. I'll get you a look at the file."

At a glance it wasn't especially promising. Kennedy was pulled over in April for driving erratically and failed the sobriety tests. The arresting officer found two handguns under the front seat and six ounces of meth in the tire well. He had two priors and when Colorado's three strikes law was explained, after he'd sobered up, he began to sing like Tom Jones, loud and long. He said he worked for a local gang boss named Shorty. He said he was in charge of a chop shop, stealing and altering cars for drug deliveries. He tipped the CPSD to two mountain properties Shorty was using to hide money and narcotics. For months the CPSD had sat outside Kennedy's wired house listening in as he played dominoes with his buddies. They had hours and hours of tapes of bullshit.

"He doesn't know much of anything or he's playing the police," Groton decided when Tanner briefed him.

"Well their plan was to seize as many assets as possible and not let another agency have access to their snitch. But Josh, you know they don't have the resources or experience to manipulate this informant and take on an operation bigger than their wildest dreams."

Tanner put in a call Sammy Moore at DEA to find out what he knew about Joe Kennedy. Moore laughed, "The CSPD's got a whole handful of nothing. They've been spending a fortune following this smalltime hood around, watching guys dig holes in the desert and listening in on dominos going click. They couldn't break a kid's lemonade ring with what they got."

"That's what I figured," Tanner said. "But I think it's likely Kennedy knows more than he shares, and I think I know how to break into that. I need to convince CSPD to hand over Kennedy to ATF and DEA."

"How?"

"We bring them in and play them the tapes of Ramon Pacheco. When they see how far along we are, I think they'll agree. We can promise them some of the assets at the end and a fat slice of the credit."

The next morning Tanner stopped at a bakery in Monument and bought two dozen donuts for his Come-to-Jesus talk with the Colorado Springs detectives. At 10:15 he took his box of cop treats and the taxi videos downstairs to the DEA offices to meet Sammy Moore and Vic Nash of the CSPD narcotics unit.

Nash was starchy polite when he showed up, dressed like a businessman instead of the scruffy "one of them" outfits of most narcotics cops. His reserve lasted about ten minutes into a choice section of the tape of Tanner's latest meeting with Ramon when he let go oedipal expletives, twice, and quickly apologized. "I can't believe it," Nash said. "He is laying out the Pacheco/Martinez organization from top to bottom." Nash ruefully wagged his head, "We haven't gotten anything like this. I'm not happy to admit it, but we haven't." He went oedipal again. "Sorry, don't like them words, but couldn't help it."

The federal agents were grinning at the detective's discomfort when there were angry shouts and crashings outside the DEA conference room, sounds like the place was being wrecked by a mob. All three rushed through the door to find it was being wrecked, not by a mob but by two officers of the law, one of whom had the other in a headlock and was smashing a fist repeatedly into his face. Tanner ran over and got both hands around Mike Reach's right wrist to stop the methodical pounding of young Colorado Springs detective Tim Carey.

"I'm going to kick that old man's ass," Carey shouted through a cut lip and a bloody nose.

"I'll show you who's old," Reach shouted back.

Nash tried to shout something at both but it came out in a croak that sounded like a frog saying motherfucker, apparently his favorite oath. Tanner and Moore shoved the brawlers into chairs and stood between them while Nash, finally able to speak coherently, kept saying only, "What is the meaning of this?"

Carey had shown up at DEA's offices and asked for a copy of the file on another investigation in which CSPD had participated but had since dropped out. Reach said that might be okay for the locals to see it but he would have to clear it "upstairs" and in any case no copy could be made and it couldn't be removed from DEA's offices. Reach then had to take a phone call and when he looked up he noticed Carey was searching through a file cabinet. Reach ordered Carey to get away from the files immediately or he would have to remove him physically.

Carey told him that CSPD was entitled to the information and that his chief of police had ordered him to return with the file. Then he added: "And I'd like to see you try to remove me, old man."

Inches shorter, twenty pounds lighter and ten years older, Reach proceeded to do that.

As Tanner said to Moore afterward, "Damn, but serving and protecting the public is fun."

"It can get interesting," Moore agreed.

Nash had become indignant, however, and was sputtering, "Is this the way you try to cooperate with local law enforcement? I'm taking this to the highest level."

Tanner put a hand on Nash's shoulder and guided him back into the conference room. "Lets just finish the tape. If this is made official neither guy comes out of it clean, especially yours. That's the way rice bowls get broken. Why don't we just call it was a training exercise and let it go at that?"

Nash was silent a minute then said, "I reckon you're right, Tanner. But I would'a put a twenty on my man." Moore gave him a shoulder squeeze, "Yeah, pardner, you could put it on his lip, stop the bleeding."

The meeting concluded without another fistfight. Nash agreed that

Tanner's investigation was far ahead of theirs and in almost a third of the time.

"In exchange for taking over Kennedy, we'll cut you in for a percentage of any assets recovered but not 100 percent. Okay?"

Fair enough," Nash agreed, "though I'm convinced Kennedy is full of it, and getting much from him except a load of crap ain't likely."

"What's next?" Moore asked as he watched Nash leave.

"I want to meet with Ramon again," Tanner said. "I want an introduction to Maria Pacheco. Then I'm going to take a chance and have Kennedy picked up. There's the gun charge against him for leverage and I want to ratchet some pressure."

Ramon Pacheco answered on the second ring.

"Sam, what's up?"

"You remember that order I told you about, needing four shorts, and some vitamins? I got to fill it and my supplier is empty." Tanner also wanted Ramon on tape delivering automatic weapons, "Any chance you can get me a full-on, one-pull?"

There was a moment of silence on the other end as Pacheco thought it over. "The vitamins are easy," he said. "We talking half-L.B. package?"

"Right."

"I can do that," Pacheco said. "But the full-on could be tough. Let me make some calls."

"How soon before I can take delivery? My buyer's out of state and antsy."

Ramon considered, "Give me until five, swing by my place in your cab. Something wrong with my SUV's starter. I'll sit in the back this time so the neighbors don't get ideas.

Tanner thought quickly. Putting Pacheco in the back seat where he'd have an edge was unacceptable. "No get in the front. Don't do anything different. Besides, who'd care?"

Tanner rang off and went into Groton's office, explaining he'd asked for four sawed-off break-opens and an automatic weapon, along with a half pound of meth. "It's going to cost four hundred for the shotguns, seven grand for the meth, dunno 'bout the auto."

Groton whistled and pushed the intercom to ask Sue the office manager about cash on hand.

"We've got about $15,000 in the safe and that's the budget for the month. We shouldn't need more than that except for what you guys are planning on buying your wives for Christmas," She deadpanned.

"Funny," Groton said. "Get $12,000 for Sam."

Tanner put the money in his briefcase and went to his office to put on a western-cut plaid shirt, old jeans and gold-and-purple lizard skin cowboy boots that Sally rated in worst taste than most of his jokes. He holstered his 9.mm, looked himself over in his door mirror and figured he was tops in lowlife chic.

Charlie Gadsen was newly back from medical leave and wanted to shadow his meeting with Ramon Pacheco. Tanner was happy for the backup. "Set up an audio receiver in your car and keep within shouting distance. I'm pretty sure I have his confidence but here's where it could go bad if I'm wrong. Tanner said the buy would be made in a Safeway parking lot a mile from Pacheco's house. "You be there ahead of me."

"Love those boots," Ramon said first thing as he got in the cab.

"You'd be surprised, some don't."

"Only in America," Ramon said dismissively. "Try 'em next country south," then he laughed, "but you could wind up barefoot."

It went easy as a burp in church. The young dealer had his half-pound of meth, a Ruger and an Orvis over and under sawed-off, a shortened Stoeger coach gun and, sadly to see, a Winchester 21 with eight inches chopped off the barrel and two from the butt. Ramon then pulled the wrap off a Type3 AK-47 and waited for the whistle. Tanner obliged him.

"Damn, you did good."

"Guy walked in with it just after lunch. Asked an ounce for it, gave him a half."

Tanner smiled, "No favor there."

"That ain't my business. I deal drugs, I deal guns, I don't deal favors."

The video hidden in the taxi meter got every word. Ramon was free and happy today with ten grand in his pockets, but he was so cooked.

"But maybe you'd do me a favor," Tanner asked after he passed over the cash. "You know some guy JoJo Kennedy, fat older dud, red faced?"

"Yeah I do, matter fact, what's up?"

"Understand he's asked questions about me. You said anything to him about our doing some business?"

"Fuck no, man. He's one of Shorty's. He does car alterations, deliveries for my father-in-law. I don't talk about you with nobody and he's the last guy I'd say anything to if I did. What I'd like to do is mess him up some. Hey, him looking at you, maybe you'd be a help there."

Tanner managed not to let anything show, but it was a laugh for later how the good guy and the bad guy could have overlapping aims. What he said was, "That could be where we start."

13

Driving home, Tanner mulled over his options with Kennedy in the case that daily revealed the criminal activity infesting Colorado Springs. Although he'd grown up in Northern Virginia when his father was transferred to Washington, D.C., he'd been born in Denver and considered Colorado his native ground. As a kid he'd longed to return to what he remembered as a mystical place of mountains, cowboys, Indians, rattlesnakes and antelopes. He hadn't imagined it with urban sprawl and criminal activity like a Chicago, L.A. or New York.

When he told Groton about his disillusionment, the RAC reminded him that Colorado was largely lawless before statehood and wasn't much gentrified by it for half a century after that. The miners that came and worked the Rockefeller steel interests around Pueblo and the whores and hoods that followed kept things rowdy well into the 20th century. When the workings of La Cosa Nostra were exposed in Senate hearings in the 1950s, the only Don from a small town listed in the organizational chart was one from Pueblo, a member of the mafia's national council.

"This state went from Cheyenne and Arapahos to Cosa Nostra and robber barons, and now it's meth heads and pocket-picking televangelists, plus a generation of vets with four tours of battle trauma," said Groton. "Hard to know when was the wilder times. Tell you what, there's lots more guns per capita all over this land, from sea to shining sea, than there ever were during westward ho. We got just over 300 million Americans now, and there are something like 300 million guns in American hands. That's fact, not a guess. Course it don't work out one for one, 'cause I got six and you got a couple, and old Ramon Pacheco appears to have a couple hundred handy. That idiot preacher I heard on the radio other day boasted of a bunch in his gun safe and one under his pillow."

Tanner had to grin. "Sometimes I think the key bureau in this area should be the Springs, not Denver. We've got L.A. gangsters, Mexican-American drug cartels, gun runners by the hundreds, looks like. Some of it, the gun aspect, is generated by the military. Before this case is over we have a chance of disrupting the largest meth and gun operation ever known in the West."

"Uh-huh, and still we're pissing in the wind."

Tanner's plan was for Kennedy to be his path to the Martinez brothers. He couldn't use Ramon given the animosity between the two factions. If he could get close to the elusive Shorty Martinez, he'd have enough for prosecutors to file charges from Colorado to California.

Taylor Rush sat in an old pickup in front of an empty house. He had a ladder and a toolbox in the bed and a magnetic sign on each door that said P&D Construction. He was watching the front door of a rancher at the end of the block, the home of JoJo Kennedy. He had a Nikon with a telephoto lens that he aimed at an old red Chevy Blazer parked in Kennedy's driveway. He took a picture and called in the plates. An hour went by and Rush got the ladder and leaned it against the side of the vacant house, from where he could still see Kennedy's house. He pounded some nails into the gable, climbed down and had a cup of coffee, leaving the driver side door casually open. Periodically he climbed the ladder and made noise with his hammer. By noon three vehicles had pulled up to Kennedy's house, disgorging two scruffy young men and a skinny woman in tight jeans. None stayed more than fifteen minutes. He snapped a shot of each of their license plates. Four hours into the stakeout the young CSPD officer called Tanner.

"Man, this dude is doing business right here. How long you want me to stay? We could bust him all over again." While he talked another car stopped at Kennedy and a woman holding a child walked to the door. "Now we got a druggie with a Jones so strong she takes her baby to get her fix. I'm hatin' this sonofabitch."

"Hang in another hour and keep taking pictures," Tanner said.

"If he leaves, follow. Did it look like anyone came out with a duffle or package that could hold weapons?"

"The last dud did, a well-built black guy. Got his picture and car number."

"Great. Has Kennedy stuck his head out the door to check the street?"

"Nope. I think the arrogant prick has been doing this so long he thinks he can't get nailed. He must believe he has us under his thumb, by us I mean our narcotics unit."

"He's going to think differently," Tanner said. "Stick with him until three and then you swing by here. Buy you a beer."

Tanner hung up and went to Groton's office. "Got a minute?" he asked, plopping in a chair. "I'm going to move a bit quicker on Kennedy. Rush has been out there all day watching him deal from his house in broad daylight."

Groton looked unhappy. "This guy doesn't sound like someone the Martinez brothers would want to spend much time with. He's way too visible. And he led the CSPD and DEA nowhere at all."

Tanner nodded. "Yeah, and I'm not going to let him fuck us over like he has the other agencies. Early in the morning I'm knocking on his door.

At 10 p.m. Tanner and Rush drove by Kennedy's house and saw no lights inside and no car in his driveway. Rush parked his surveillance truck where he'd been that morning, and they settled to wait until dawn. They'd watch for Kennedy's return, see if he came with company, and if alone they'd rouse him at 6 a.m. They hadn't applied for a warrant because it was a friendly visit though Kennedy likely wouldn't consider it so.

At 1:35 a.m. headlights shown down the street and the beat-up Blazer turned into Kennedy's drive. The door popped open and Kennedy stepped out, weaving his way across the lawn. He was alone. At 6 a. m. the officers stood either side of Kennedy's door, unholstered their sidearm's and knocked hard. They heard mumbling and then a curse as someone tripped and a voice inside called, "Who the fuck is it?"

"Open the door. This is agent Tanner from ATF."

"Well it's six in the fucking morning. Can't you come back?"

"Open the door, please," Tanner replied, "If you have a weapon, put it on the floor and kick it out when you open the door. Otherwise my partner, Agent Rush here, might take it as a threatening gesture and have to remove your brains."

The door opened slowly and Tanner heard metal hit the floor and a pistol came sliding out the door. Kennedy stepped back hands up as the officers entered.

"Lets go to the kitchen and you can brew us some coffee," Tanner said. "Then we can have a pleasant conversation about how you can avoid going on the five-year jailhouse diet by helping us a whole lot."

Kennedy said nothing and led the way.

"Did the CPSD explain that from now on you would be my itch to scratch?"

"Yeah. But I don't know if I can help. What is it you want?" Kennedy poured water and grounds in the pot and plugged it in. "Cream or sugar?"

"Black," Tanner said. "And here's the thing. You been dicking around with the CSPD boys and DEA for weeks and produced zip. Those days are gone. Now you will produce viable information. I want connections to the meth and gun and stolen auto trade that you have been running with impunity, and you have two days to satisfy me."

Kennedy started to talk and Tanner raised a hand. "I don't mean to be unfriendly here. Let me tell you a story, in your case more of a parable. A guy dies and goes to hell. The devil appears and assures him he'll find things to his liking. On Monday, the devil says, he can eat all the finest foods, on Tuesday he can imbibe the best wines, on Wednesday all the drugs he wants, and every Thursday there's an orgy with the most beautiful women imaginable. Then the devil says, 'By the way are you gay?' and the man responds no. Devil says, 'Then you're not going to like Friday.'"

Tanner stared hard at the fat man until he looked away. "Mister Kennedy, you begin giving me your utmost cooperation right away, or three days from now you'll begin spending your nights with about 500 men so horny they'd fuck the crack of dawn."

Tanner stood up and leaned over the table and put his face about three inches from Kennedy. "Two days," he said, and he left.

14

"How long is this going to take? I have some business downtown."

It was 11 a.m. Kennedy had a day old beard and reeked of whiskey and sweat. The stale cigarette smell in the room made Tanner's nose burn. But the man's arrogance nearly made him laugh.

"Well you know, that sort of depends on you," he replied. Tanner plopped a blue nylon bag on the kitchen table, pulled out a set of waist chains and leg irons and dropped them on the coffee table.

"I'm here to collect and if I don't get what I want, you're going to put these on and your business downtown will be different than you planned." Tanner looked at Kennedy and made a face. "Jesus, you smell. Take a shower before we do anything. I don't want you fouling my car."

He followed Kennedy into the bathroom to make sure there was no way out. A small window sat over the tub but no way was Kennedy's ass squeezing through it. Tanner settled in an overstuffed chair in a corner away from the unmade bed while the dealer washed.

When Kennedy came out in a towel that wouldn't reach all the way around him, Tanner said, "Sit on the bed and I'll get your clothes." He rummaged through the closet and drawers and found underwear, size fifty jeans and the man's cleanest dirty shirt. When Kennedy was dressed Tanner tossed the irons on his bed and said, "Put these on."

"Wait a minute," Kennedy whined. "I thought I was getting a chance to help you."

"You are. But they'll remain on you if what you give me is as bad as what you've been feeding CSPD. I have you on gun and dope charges that kick in the habitual act, so you could spend the rest of your years bending over for bigger guys. Your choice."

Kennedy reluctantly put the chain around his waist and fastened the clasp. Tanner put the handcuffs on him and fastened them to the chain.

"Looks right on you," the agent said. "So before we go uptown, what do you have?"

"I can give you this bigshot from Texas who has been a major player here, distributing for Maria Pacheco. You know her name?"

"Yep."

"Well this dude has a distribution crew of more than forty." His mouth was wet and Kennedy wanted to wipe it then realized he couldn't with his hands cuffed. "Look, you can take these off. I can put you next to a lieutenant I'm friends with, guy named Roy Crowe.

"That's a start. Let's meet," Tanner said

"It'll take a few days."

Tanner grabbed the waist chain and pulled Kennedy toward the door. "Agent Rush give me a hand here," he shouted out the door.

As Rush appeared in the doorway, Kennedy almost collapsed. "No! No! I can call him today and get back to you this afternoon. I'm cooperating."

Tanner waved Rush back and let go of the waist chain. He pointed to the telephone on an end table near the front room sofa. "Fuck this afternoon, JoJo. Call him now," he said. "You tell him Jack from Topeka wants to meet him, right away."

He passed his cell phone to Kennedy, who tried to dial, muffed it and had to started over. His hands were shaking.

"Roy, JoJo. Yeah, I'm okay. Sorry to bother but I have an old friend in from Topeka looking for action. I vouch for him. This afternoon all right?" There was a long pause. "Okay. I'll call tomorrow and see if we can't set up something.

Turning to Tanner, Kennedy said, "He's not available this afternoon, maybe tomorrow."

"Where does he live?" Kennedy gave the address and Tanner took the chain off his waist. "Here is what's going to happen. I will be in touch every day. If I think you have called this guy back to warn him, it's over. You'd better work hard for my introduction. Time's short."

He put his chains back in the bag. He sat back in the overstuffed chair and crossed a leg. "Now let's talk some about your chop shop, and you can tell me about hiding ephedrine buried in the mountains."

Dinner with Mama was generally an ordeal for Ramon Pacheco. For one thing she really couldn't cook, and he always wondered how anybody could mess up something as basic as *cosina de la familia Mexicana*. Also, she was grumpy about the continued absence of her lover and enforcer Manny Saurez, who suddenly had flown back to Mexico at the time of Tirado's murder leading Ramon to suspect a connection. He knew not to voice his suspicions to his mother. The less he knew the better. Then too, he figured his mama was just naturally grumpy, never considering it was himself provoking grumpiness in her.

He meant to coax. She heard wheedling.

"Sam can be an important asset for us," Ramon said. "Sam wants to meet with you."

"Sam, Sam," said Maria.

Her boy was determined to bring in this man and didn't even know his last name. She sipped her *rioja* and said nothing for a moment, holding the glass in front of her watching the shimmer in the light of the small table lamp. It is good wine, she thought, and this is a good boy. He just wasn't so much a man even at thirty. She felt a flush of anger as she thought how her son's father-in-law had stolen the hunk of her business. Her anger over Ramon' miscalculations about his in-laws and his treacherous, spoiled wife would never go away, and it showed in her response to his taxi-driving amigo from somewhere in Kansas.

"I have no need to bring him close," she said. "We have lost Tirado and Rahall, too, because of mistakes made directly under you." Her voice was low but its tone sharp, and Ramon looked down at his plate."

"I know, I know. Am I never going to get from under this, Mama?"

The pain in his voice softened her anger. She reached across the table and touched his head, smoothing down his hair.

"Do you know his full name? "

"You know the rule is first names only," he said, "until there is meaningful trust."

"And I have no reason to trust or distrust him," she replied. "And I do not want to meet him until he has done something to merit my trust. He is yours to trust." And she paused. "Or not."

The warning wasn't lost on Ramon. He hadn't admitted to his mother how much about their organization he had revealed to Tanner. If this turned out badly, he knew her tolerance would stop and he would be looking over his shoulder for Manny Suarez. He hadn't seen Manny for weeks and he believed this suggested his mother's protector had something to do with Tirado's death. That meant that his mother had ordered it.

Changing the subject, he said, "Martinez and his brothers are digging holes all over the landscape."

"How do you know this?"

"My taxi driver tells me JoJo Kennedy has been blabbing about mountain expeditions. What you bet they are burying ephedrine from the vitamin company everywhere, picking it up when they need it."

"Kennedy?"

"Yeah. He is a fat drunk the Martinez's use for smalltime errands and entertainment. He also boosts cars and moves them through some organization I have not got a handle on."

"I know of this one," said Maria, "but not so much. You have been keeping your eyes open and that is more like it. Maybe the taxi guy is useful, if he can come up with that information."

Ramon smiled at her praise and change of tone. "I told you he has a lot of connections. He caught Kennedy snooping around his business and he didn't like it, so he reached out. Also, he paid me well for some product and guns for a special order in Kansas."

"Bueno. Be careful with this man but let me know what else you find out. I think soon there will come a time when we resolve our differences with your in-laws. I did not climb out of the bars of Juarez to be put back there by these *hijos de puta*."

Tanner sat outside the house of Roy Crowe, age thirty-one and previously of Austin, in a middle class neighborhood in north Colorado Springs. He was behind the wheel of an old brown Buick used for surveillance but too clapped-out for pursuit. Tanner had a six-pack of

Bud on the seat beside him, and he wore a wire. Josh Groton was parked in a follow car on the block behind him.

Since leaving Kennedy that morning Tanner had run a background on Crowe and found two arrests for armed robbery in Oklahoma that had been dismissed, a drug and gun possession charge from Texas still pending, and a couple of assault beefs dropped when the complainant failed to show up. There were no priors suggesting major drug use. He plainly wasn't the worst bad boy and likely was somebody's second banana.

Tanner planned to show up unannounced at Crowe's door and start a friendly conversation about how each could help the other. Before he could get out of the Buick he saw a skinny man with short-cut sandy hair come out of a side door. From wrap sheet photos he had gotten from Criminal Investigation Network, he recognized Crowe, though the man looked much less formidable in person. He wore a nylon jacket over a polo shirt and chinos. He was in fact fairly natty for someone in a line of work where cowboy duds or motorcycle leathers were the norm.

Tanner grabbed the beer six-pack and jumped out of his car before Crowe could reach his.

"Excuse me," he called, walking fast up the driveway. "I'm the guy JoJo called about this morning. I'm Jack." Tanner was smiling broadly, thrusting out his right hand. I apologize but I'm suddenly having to leave town this afternoon, and I thought I'd take a chance on meeting you, talk about maybe doing business." He held out the six-pack, "Have a couple brews?"

Crowe frowned, "How you know my house?"

Tanner looked surprised, "Well Kennedy, he said. . ."

"That fat fuck." Crowe was pissed, but Tanner was friendly and Kennedy had been insistent on the phone. He hesitated then said, "I tried to tell JoJo I have to go out this afternoon. But you're here and I can use a beer, I'll give it a few minutes, come on in."

"Cool," Tanner said. "Don't want to impose, just get acquainted and tell you about myself and what I'm looking for. Kennedy says you're the guy to see and some guy from Texas. He didn't mention the dude's name and I don't care, if you can handle this yourself."

Crowe led him into a large rec room with a bar and fireplace and an arrangement of white leather couches. Opening the beers and handing Tanner one, he said, "Haven't seen you around. Where you from?"

"I was born here but I do my business mostly in Oklahoma and Kansas, and the Texas panhandle."

"What kind of business?"

"A little this and a lot of that." Tanner said, smiling big. "Buy product here, the metal kind, sell it out of state. Right now I have a sudden call for a quantity of chemical rejuvenator and I'm having trouble coming up with it."

"What's the call?" Crowe finished his beer and sat it down on a coffee table. "You ready for another?"

"Not yet," Tanner said and he went for broke. "Fifty LBs," he said, looking steadily at Crowe, knowing it would get his attention. It did.

The dealer was about to take a swig but brought the bottle down from his lips and whistled. "Whoa! We're talking major value."

"I know. I've got a Kansas buyer that will take that plus a shipment of hardware on a fairly regular basis. He retails it at prices you wouldn't believe. But we need a regular supplier."

"We?"

"I don't work exclusively with him but he's been taking more and more of what I can get. Now I need a new supplier. I don't want the cooking business and neither does he. About a month ago, his major cooker in Missouri was busted by ATF and DEA. Maybe you read about it?"

Tanner was fairly sure Crowe knew about the raid. It made the nightly news and even The New York Times. And when a supply is interrupted anywhere the network hums.

"Yeah, I do know about it," Crowe said. "The guy was a top drawer chemist, from what I heard was cooking "peanut butter meth" He glanced at his watch. "Listen, I have to go out. I don't know exactly what we can do for you, but I will talk to my principle. It's a lot of cash. You sure you can manage it?"

"No problem," Tanner said rising and placing his empty second bottle on the bar. "I'll be in touch soon."

They shook hands and Tanner headed for the stairway to the first floor. He turned at the stairway and pulled out a notepad, scratched something on it and walked back to Crowe. "Here's my cell phone number. Give me an answer in a couple of days or sooner."

He went up the stairs and out to the Buick, where he murmured, "Get that, Josh?"

"Oh yeah," came the reply. "You'll be hearing from him. Let's head for the barn."

15

Over the next week Tanner met twice with Roy Crowe, buying eight ounces of meth and three pistols. His order for fifty pounds went unfilled. Crowe claimed the man above him he called Jay Ray was away in Texas because of a family health problem. Tanner couldn't be sure whether he was being stalled or his order was too much for Jay Ray's crew.

Then Crowe called his cell to say Jay Ray was back and wanted to meet, and Tanner had to stall. Sally and both girls were sick with the flu, running high fevers, and he'd have to stay home and wipe noses and heat chicken soup.

"Can't make it just now," Tanner said, and lied, "I'm making a run over to Kansas City. Be tied up there a few days. Call you soon as I'm heading back."

Then he rang Josh Groton to ask for an agent to drive by Crowe's address to run a check on any car there with Texas plates. "Hell check the plates of every car on the block if we have to," he urged. "I think we'll ID his superior."

"Everybody's out, I'll do it myself," Groton said.

A half hour later he drove slowly by Crowe's house in a Chrysler with a six-liter Hemi V-8 and tinted windows, a model favored by gang-bangers and in fact was confiscated by the agency from a St. Louis drug thug.

He noted a late model Toyota SUV with the name of a Ft. Worth dealer on the plate holder and Texas tags. He rolled slowly to the end of the street, made a U-turn at the intersection and passed by again, pausing to get the number jotted on a pad attached to his dash. He no sooner put the pen away in the visor than a tall man in a sweatshirt came running out of the garage and jumped into the SUV.

"Woops," Groton said out loud. "Believe I stepped on his dick."

He pressed his accelerator and the big car laid a strip of rubber, pushing sixty in seven seconds. He touched the brakes at the first intersection and cut the wheel sharply, turned right for a short block then back left at the next street.

The chasing SUV teetered and fish-tailed through both turns. The driver managed to bring it back and floored the accelerator to try to keep up with the big sedan. Groton grinned, enjoying the chase after too long driving a desk. They turned onto a parkway where the interceptor was capable of speeds the Toyota couldn't match, but Groton was having too much fun to just pull away. He saw a break in the median strip ahead and barely touching his brakes whipped the wheel left and right again to ease through it. Just as he decided to run away from this jerk his driver's side mirror disintegrated."

Jesus! The idiot was shooting. Groton stomped his emergency brake and spun the steering wheel hard around left, and the car skidded in a clean 180 to point back at the car in pursuit. Groton drew his 9 mm with his left hand, aimed it out his window and squeezed two quick shots that punctured the Toyota's windshield.

The white SUV cut to the right and sped past, the driver so far down in the seat only the top of his head showed. As it went by, Groton pointed the Glock but didn't fire. "Bye, Bye," he said and watched his rearview mirror as the car made it to the next intersection, turned and sped away.

The few other cars on the street had pulled over, obviously frightened. Groton noticed two of the drivers holding cell phones out, undoubtedly calling 911.

He switched on the car's radio and called CSPD. He identified himself and said he had been in pursuit of a felon. "Dispatcher. Tell your street boys I'm in a company car on the parkway between 39th and 40th and have pulled over. I'll wait here with my credentials."

When three CSPD patrol cars rolled up lights flashing, Groton was standing outside the car leaning on the fender smoking a cigar and holding his badge high for them to see.

"Sorry about this, boys." Groton said. "I was doing a bit of surveillance work on a major case when one of those under investigation started after me in an SUV. I was about to shake him when he took a shot at me." He pointed at his smashed driver's side mirror.

"But someone reported more than one shot, Agent Groton," said a cop who had recognized him.

"Yeah. Well I put two into his windshield. Had to do something. And I hate those bigass SUVs.

Jay Ray Marsh screamed into his cell phone trying to maneuver the white Toyota with one hand and hold the phone to his ear with the other at a high rate of speed. "Some fucker almost blew my head off."

"Who was it?" asked Crowe on the other end of the line. He was trying to keep his own voice low and even, hoping to calm Marsh.

"I haven't got a fucking clue," Marsh shouted, glancing at the rear view mirror. "He doesn't seem to be following, but I'm not coming to your place. Keep an eye out and call me if you see a black Chrysler. I'm headed to my place." He closed the clamshell, turned left and headed for his penthouse. When he drove into the parking lot he noticed Sherry Sanford's Dodge Viper was parked in the space next to his. She had her own place but also a key to his. He wasn't in the mood for her, with two bullet holes in the windshield.

He pulled the Toyota next to the Viper, got out and picked up a loose brick at the corner of the parking garage. He looked around to see if anyone was watching and quickly smashed the brick down shattering the glass and wiping out evidence of the bullet holes. He pitched the brick through the broken window and into the car and left it there, he then took out his knife and dug the slugs from the headrest of the front passenger seat

Sherry met him at the door of his apartment, wearing jeans and a purple silk shirt tied at the waist. She was a tall dark-haired girl with wide-set deep blue eyes and dancer's legs. She'd been in the trade off and on and had used a variety of chemicals but somehow had maintained her figure and avoided the wear and tear on her complexion.

"I've had a problem," he said before she could say hello. "It's on a need-to-know basis and you don't need to know." He took her head in his hands, kissed her and pushed her away. "You need to take off now and call later. Right now I got business." She started to protest but knew better, shrugged and walked to the elevator.

"Ta, ta," she said softly, holding up her hand and waving without turning around.

Marsh watched the tight jeans cupping her bottom, a connoisseur's regard, and closed the door. He called Crowe. "Anything?"

"No. I haven't taken my eyes off the street. But I've been thinking, whoever it was has probably been looking for me."

He wanted to say Marsh provoked the incident by flying out the door in pursuit. But like Sherry, he also knew better.

Marsh let a silence stretch then said, "Why don't you come over here, we'll figure it out over drinks. I need to work out how soon I can get the window fixed without a lot of attention."

Crowe was cautious on the drive over, pulling to the roadside several times survey the traffic, once watching for five minutes to see if anyone also stopped and waited.

"That dude could drive," Marsh said as they sat at his bar sipping Luksusowa potato vodka. "He could have gotten away from me. But it was like he was playing with me. I took a shot and he did a 180 and came straight at me. Thirty yards away he put two rounds in the passenger side of the windshield."

Crowe thought a minute and said, "You can't have a chase and shootout in broad daylight without the cops knowing. Do we have anyone close to the cops we could ask about it?"

Marsh shook his head and poured himself a fresh drink, shaking the glass a little to make the ice jiggle. "We used to but not now."

"Well, what I'm thinking is this could be somebody working with the Martinez's. I can't see Ramon Pacheco snooping on us, but the Martinez's maybe yeah."

Marsh stood up and went into the bathroom without comment. When he returned he had a Walther PPK stuck in his waistband and he motioned Crowe to come with him.

"Is that the piece you used to shoot at the car," Crowe said

"Yeah, I had to hit the can when I came back and laid it down on the edge of tub and forgot it."

Crowe said, "Jay Ray, you need some serious chillin.' I have no idea why anybody would be sniffing around, but I think you need to talk to Ramon. If the Martinez's are making a play, he should get a heads up."

Marsh nodded and dialed. "There has been an incident," he reported when Ramon answered. "Crowe and I are on the way over. Don't leave."

"The guy was definitely watching the house," Marsh said, studying Pacheco for any sign he knew about it.

Ramon looked startled. "Who could it be? I know that Shorty is capable but the thing is going well, why would he mess it up?"

"How about your mother?" Crowe asked. "We're the key to her distribution now. She got doubts about us?"

Ramon thought a minute and shook his head. "She needs your operation. I don't think she'd be using anybody who'd draw attention to it. In any case it looks to me like someone was checking out you, not Marsh."

Marsh agreed. Maria had reached out to him, asking him to take up the slack after losing Rahall and Tirado, and he was buying her product by the pound. It had to be the Martinez family getting ready to apply pressure.

"What about this guy Jack from Kansas City?" Marsh wondered.

"Hasn't been around," said Crowe. "Said he'd be back this weekend. What we going to do about his wanting fifty pounds?"

"We can do business if he has the cash," Marsh said. "But that's a lot of product for a first-time buy. You set up a meeting to sell him some smaller amount and promise the major order next time. I want to see how quick he comes with the cash."

16

"James Raymond Marsh, born 10-30-80, Arlington, Texas, last known address, 342 South 49th Street, Apartment 29, Colorado Springs. Friends call him Jay Ray." Groton pushed the paper across his desk to Tanner.

"This is our guy," he said. "Never even been arrested, no juvies nor even traffic busts. How does a guy like this dude have a clean rap sheet? He sure as hell came after me with no thought at all."

Tanner shook his head. "Kennedy said he only knew the guy as the Texan. He couldn't give me more. Roy Crowe did the same, but sure as shit knows the guy's name. He indicated the guy is a tough customer who reacts violently when cornered. But for a supposed badass, he got scared off kind of quick. You know, Arlington is a pretty upscale area and this could be some spoiled rich kid."

Groton smiled. "And here's a backgrounder from the Dallas office," and shoved it across the desk. "His daddy's a state judge, mama's a realtor, and he went to SMU on a football scholarship, which he lost his sophomore year and went on academic probation. I'd bet that's when he got involved with drugs. He managed to get his marketing degree, was hired on by Katie Cookies and was sent to manage their plant in Colorado Springs a year and a half ago. He walked out of the plant, giving no notice at all, late last year. Guess he found a fulltime opportunity in methamphetamine."

"Another kind of baked goods," Tanner laughed, "and it does pay better than cookies. Though it's a business where terminations have a whole different meaning. I can't help it, I'm going to be thinking of this guy as the cookie monster."

As Groton and Tanner looked at the case now, it was moving on two tracks, one with Ramon that lead to his mother and the Martinez brothers, one from Kennedy that led through Crowe and Marsh toward the Martinez's.

"It's the cookie monster I want to concentrate on for right now," Tanner said. "I'm calling Crowe to say I got back early and push him for a quick buy and maybe a face to face with Marsh."

Crowe didn't answer his cell until after noon, said he was sleeping in and sick.

"Sorry 'bout that," Tanner said, "but I'm back and I really need to have a sit-down with you or your chief. No offense, but let's do business or I'll take my suitcase and leave." He knew that Crowe understood the suitcase was code for cash.

"Don't get sore," Crowe said. "We're ready to go and why don't you come by my place tonight around eight o'clock, meet my partner. I'm not sure we can give you fifty pounds but three or four to start. Also got some high-powered friends for you to meet."

Tanner understood the friends were weapons. "Sounds alright," he said and hung up. Then he dialed Ramon.

"I'll pick you up in the Taxi for a cup of coffee and some information about a deal I'm cooking up."

Tanner was operating in the belief that Marsh was in the pay of the Martinez's and didn't link directly to Ramon and Maria Pacheco. If they did however, then his undercover identities as Sam the Taxi Driver and Jack from Kansas could get snarled.

Ramon was on the curb waiting when Tanner pulled up to his house.

"I promised to buy from you and that hasn't changed," Tanner told him "But I got wind of another supply network run by some dude from Texas. I met one of his guys, tall, thin, preppy looking, named Crowe."

Pacheco grinned, something he didn't do often. "You buy from them, you're buying from us."

Tanner felt blood drain from his face. JoJo Kennedy had misdirected him, giving up a Pacheco lieutenant instead of a direct link to the Martinez organization. Kennedy's cutie move was going to cost him his freedom by day's end.

Tanner tried not to show how surprised he was, but had to ask, "How does that work?"

"The Texan is a guy named Jay Ray Marsh. He's got his own crew, works directly for my mother. I don't like him and I stay away from him. Marsh can be scary and my mother uses him because right now she has no choice. So far, he has been straight with us. He showed up at my place Saturday demanding to know if we had put surveillance on him. Seems someone was casing Crowe's place and Marsh took it personally and went after the guy."

"So what happened?" Tanner asked, making his eyes wide with feigned excitement.

"Well the guy out-drove him and turned his ass inside out. I told my mother about it and she ordered me to stay completely away from him. This guy comes unglued under pressure. If we could find another distributor. . ." He gave Tanner an inquiring look.

"Nah, I'm strictly a middleman buyer. But if you don't want to be around this guy neither do I. If he turns on you though, you can count on me watching your back."

When he dropped Pacheco back at his house, Tanner knew he was playing a seriously risky game. If the parallel paths of his undercover work crossed, it could put him in a pucker fast. But he was convinced that wholesale arrests were only a few weeks away.

Sherry Sanford drove the Interstate south toward Fountain, the black Viper doing 100 with only slight pressure on the pedal. It was 3 a.m. and traffic was light. The Highway Patrol had few cars out at this hour and she knew that. Jay Ray's snores had rattled her out of a deep sleep and after she'd peed she recognized a serious Jones for meth. She knew a supplier who'd stay open all night and she dressed quickly, letting herself out of Marsh's penthouse.

She got to the Fountain turnoff almost before she realized it and hit the exit ramp fast, just managing to hold the car through a turn onto the main drag. A red light flashed behind her and a patrol car sounded a quick woop-woop. She considered running but figured she could talk her way out, certain there was nothing in the car to incriminate her. She pulled to the curb across from a strip mall, completely dark and quiet.

"License and registration," the officer ordered, shining his flashlight full in her face and holding it there. She squinted into the glare and noticed he was in the tan uniform of a sheriff's deputy.

She passed the registration and he examined it at arm's length, then leaned close, a hand on his gun butt, to sniff for any scent of liquor.

"You know how fast you came off that ramp?" he demanded. She answered in a timid voice, "No sir, I actually turned off at the last minute rather than drive to Pueblo where I have relatives. I was sleepy and looking for some place to get coffee."

"Well, it was over 60 when you hit the exit ramp."

"Oh! Sorry, I didn't see the exit until the last minute," she lied.

He went back to his car and turned on the interior light. She could see him pick up his radio and call in her license and registration. It was an edgy ten minutes before he returned with her papers."

"There's an all night diner about a half mile down the street here, and I want you to follow me to it."

She followed him driving slow, and checked him over as he got out of his car. Tall, broad shoulders, small butt, slim waist, haircut long for a cop, about thirty. *This might be interesting*, she was thinking.

"I'm Deputy Ray Ballard, Miss Sanford," he said as they reached the diner's steps. "I'm going to buy you some coffee and perhaps something to eat and we're going to talk for a while."

"Is this usual?" she asked.

He regarded her a moment, letting her see his eyes wander over her.

"If I give you a ticket it'll be for more than speeding. Most likely it would be Driving Under the Influence, of something."

She started to protest but thought better of it and she walked through the door he was holding open.

"Hi Doris," he said the woman behind the counter and guided Sherry to a booth in the back. He took off his Stetson and he waited until she took her seat across from him before he sat. Then he held her gaze with his bright blue eyes and smiled.

A gentleman and, she understood at once, the department pretty boy.

He handed her a menu and said, "I'm having something substantial and I suggest you do the same." She got it, if he didn't charm he'd coerce. She ordered bacon and eggs, with home fries, same as him.

When Doris brought their orders, he said, "May I call you Sherry?"

"Please."

"I have a proposition for you."

Her eyebrows lifted at the word.

"No, no," he said. "Here's what I mean. I think you're going to visit relatives down the road at 3:30 a.m. I think you've been drinking, a little, and doing some other interesting chemicals, just going by the dilation of your eyes, and the hour of course. Then when I called in, your record pops up an arrest for suspicion of prostitution, but no conviction. So I've got to ask you, what are you really doing out here?"

Pretty Boy hadn't bought her first lie so she gave him another.

"The truth is, I was at my boyfriend's and he had a friend over, and then at a certain point he wanted me to do his friend, too, and I wasn't in the mood and he got abusive and I got the hell out. I'm just taking a ride, to let off some steam, and it happens I do have a girlfriend in Pueblo and I thought I could ring her if I got that far." She smiled and gave him the look, "Then you came along and saved me, it's that simple."

It wasn't that simple and whether he believed her or not, he said, "I believe you."

They ate in silence until plates were clean and she said, "So what's the proposition?"

She looked at her watch, now showing half past four. Two pickups with hunters pulled into the parking lot. "If you're going to continue to be a nice guy and not arrest me, I truly need to get back to Colorado Springs at a safe rate of speed."

He nodded. "Here it is. I want your eyes. If you know or hear of anything I can use to whack the drug trade in the Fountain area, I want you to let me know. I'm betting you can do that. Will you do that?"

"What's in it for me?"

"I have colleagues in law enforcement, colleagues who could make life uncomfortable. You wouldn't go out for the evening without maybe being bothered with something. I don't like doing that so I'll tell you now, I don't need you to rat on close friends, just give me a break now and then."

She thought for almost a minute. "First of all I'm not into anything heavy," she lied. "But I do hear things. I can be a good citizen. I have to say this, you're sexy. Married?"

He shook his head no.

"Then, tentatively, I accept the proposition. But please don't say my name to anyone. I don't want to end up in a mountain ravine." She took a $20 bill and put it on the table. "For the breakfast." And she stood up.

He handed it back, "This is on me." He put a card with his name and address and phone numbers on it in her hand.

She put it in her billfold and dropped that in her purse. She didn't intend to give it another thought.

17

Eight p.m., rain pelted and winds moaned down the mountains biting the skin when Tanner arrived at Crowe's door. He was wired, backed up by Groton and Charlie Gadsen in separate cars and DEA agents Sammy Moore and Mike Reach in two other vehicles.

Crowe apologized as soon as he opened his door. "You're right on time but we're in the middle of a distribution." He led the way down a short flight into the wide recreation room where about forty people milled around, some with drinks, none with a smile or nod.

Crowe showed him through the sullen groups into a side office and shut the door. "When I told you eight o'clock I didn't know Jay Ray was going to get started that early with this. He wants to meet you and get some business going. We can arrange a buy for you in about an hour. Could you kill some time and come back? This bunch will be out of here then."

"Where's Jay Ray?"

"He's in another room cutting product for the distributors. We've been at it for about an hour so there isn't much more to do."

Tanner had to wonder if he were being set up. But if that were the case, why not take care of him now? Maybe too many witnesses.

"I can let myself out. I have to run an errand anyway. Is there a liquor store in the neighborhood?"

Crowe directed him to a strip mall about a mile away.

"What do you make of that?" Groton asked when Tanner pulled up next to the RAC's car a block away from the scene. "I don't know whether you should go back in there again. Maybe we ought to bust this place now."

Moore agreed. "This could be a trap. They know you're carrying money for a buy and we really don't know what these guys are capable of."

Tanner shook his head. "They smell bigger things, and I think Marsh has had a good report from Crowe. Right now they're looking at big payoffs and don't want to screw it up. I don't think there's a lot of risk here, your call, Josh."

Groton stared ahead for a moment. "We'll take the chance."

When Tanner got out of his car he walked past several distributors just leaving. They stared past him. Letting himself in, he went downstairs and found Crowe on a couch, a .357 magnum on the lamp table next to him. To his right stood a huge man, several inches taller than Tanner, weighing close to three hundred pounds, with a .45 tucked in his waistband.

Tanner took a few steps to his left away from the man with the automatic in his belt.. "Okay, Roy, what's with the hardware?"

Gadsen, nearest to house, eased his car closer. He had a bandoleer of shotgun shells hung over one shoulder and a 12 gage across his lap. His plan was to drive the car across the lawn and ram it through the front door at the first shout for help. From what he was hearing through his ear-button those could be the next words.

"Easy, easy," Groton's voice came over the radio. "He knows what he's doing. Be ready but be cool." But he too moved his car closer to the house as did the two DEA agents. "If he says 'Put the weapons down', we go."

Inside, Tanner bent over and pulled a beer from a cooler on the floor. "Who's the heavy artilleryman?" he asked Crowe.

"That's Freddy. He stays around when we're doing a split. Marsh should be finished and in here soon."

The goon with the gun stared at him and said nothing.

Tanner pulled the tab on the beer can and took a swig, moving back to his right in front of the bodyguard.

"Excuse me," he said passing in front of the man as he moved toward the sofa where Crowe sat. The bodyguard, his feet planted wide, didn't move. As he squeezed past, Tanner grabbed the 45 and pulled it quick from the bodyguard's waist. He was three feet away before the gunman reacted.

"Man, this is really a nice piece," Tanner said, holding the gun aloft and sort of waving it back and forth.

"Hey," the man said. "What the fuck you doing? Give me back my gun." He took a step toward Tanner.

"Sure," the Tanner said. "You won't need it though. This is all friendly." He popped the magazine, racked the shell out of the chamber and put the empty pistol atop a book case behind the couch. He sat down next to Crowe, and at the same time he picked up Crowe's piece from the lamp table.

"These things make me nervous, Roy," he said, putting the gun out of Crowe's reach on the opposite lamp table.

The big man took a step toward Tanner, reached on the shelf and retrieved his gun. Almost standing over the seated Tanner he loaded the magazine and racked a shell into the automatic's firing chamber.

In a low firm voice, Tanner said to Crowe without taking his eyes off of the big man. "You better get your zombie under control. I don't take kindly to someone standing over me and racking one into the chamber. To me, that's a threat."

"It's okay, Freddy," Crowe said. "Jack here is invited. He's going to be a good customer."

The big man held his ground.

Tanner's hand was an inch from the Glock under his shirt. He kept his eyes on the man for any sign of movement.

"I think you should do just exactly what Roy told you, big boy," Tanner said, an edge in his voice.

"Freddy, get the fuck out of here and tell Jay Ray we got to do some business."

When Freddy left Tanner put his briefcase flat on the coffee table but made no effort to open it.

"What do you have for me?"

Crowe picked up a bag at his feet next to the table and sat it next to the briefcase. He took out two Glocks, a Smith & Wesson .357 magnum, a Ruger P89 and Lorcin .380 and two pounds of crystal meth.

"How's this for a start?" he asked just as Jay Ray Marsh walked through the door, a tall moose-jawed man in a black silk shirt and cream Italian loafers. He had a snub nose revolver in a shoulder holster.

"Jack," said Tanner and stood up holding out his hand.

"Jay Ray," Marsh said, taking his hand and looking at him closely. "Seems you really pissed off Freddy." He grinned.

"What do you think?" he said nodding toward the guns and meth.

"Looks good," Tanner replied, " but I'm going to need a lot more. This will do as a start, though." He opened the briefcase and took out $17,000. That's a fair price. Any problem?"

"Nope," Marsh said, smiling. "How much more are you going to want?"

"Well, I told Crowe we could use 50 pounds. Say by week after next?"

"We'll have it," Marsh said. "I'll be in touch with some other deals. Crowe has your cell. I like your style, Jack. Let's do some long-term business."

He motioned Crowe to collect the money and put the guns and dope back in the bag and handed it to Tanner.

They shook hands all around and Tanner said, "Roy, give me a hand here if you can. Walk me to my car outside. If I run into your man Freddy, you should know I will kill him without hesitation."

"You needn't worry about him," Marsh said. "But, man, I do like your style."

Tanner headed for their rendezvous point—a quiet bar on the north side. He took a circuitous route and his backups made sure he wasn't followed. He'd been exhilarated but now the adrenalin faded and his limbs felt like lead. He radioed Groton, "Looked like we were going to have a dance down there."

"You almost ruined a pair of pants for me" Groton replied. "Gadsen. was ready to drive through the front door and blast away."

By the time they reached the bar, the snow clouds had formed over the mountains and tiny flakes were swirling. They were sweating in the heat of the room before their first drinks came.

"We can't let it go a lot longer," Groton said. "How do you size up what we have, Sam?"

"Right now we have Maria and Ramon Pacheco and a couple dozen of their street distributors. We got Kennedy. Now we have Crowe and Marsh on a single transaction. We got them all pointing at the three Martinez's and by monitoring the vitamin factory we're going to have them on the ephedrine end of it. Marsh looks to be a truly major cog in the whole damn thing, and until now he's been invisible to law enforcement at any level. I'd like to keep going with him to see what more we can get that leads to Maria and the extremely elusive Shorty."

"See any women in there?" Groton asked.

" No. Crowe made an off-hand mention of someone named Sherry. Says she's a looker who'd been hooked up with Marsh for a year or so but turns the occasional trick to afford some of her extravagances."

"Could we get to her?" Moore asked.

"Always a possibility, but I'd rather not chance pissing off Marsh. Right now we have one buy from Marsh on record. But one's not enough. With his non-record the dude could be out of jail before we cataloged the contraband."

"No question about it," Groton agreed. "Give it two weeks, see if we come up with something to slam the door on 'em once and for all."

"You have the right to remain silent. No, you are obligated to keep your mouth shut since nothing but bullshit comes from it. Turn around and stick out your hands."

Putting the cuffs on JoJo Kennedy was a cop's moment to savor, good as a donut. Tanner had promised himself he'd do this one himself since realizing Kennedy had given him bum info about Marsh working directly for the Martinez's.

It was the morning after his solo foray into the Marsh distribution network, and he'd had a short and restless night to reflect on how vulnerable he'd been there if anyone present had realized Kansas Jack was the same guy as Sam the Cabbie.

"You don't understand," Kennedy whined.

"No, you don't understand," Tanner shot back. "I understand that you were more afraid of Shorty than you were of me, so you pointed me wrong. Now you are having a learning moment. Which is, you have a right to a lawyer, and every goddamn thing you say I am personally holding against you. So. Shut. Up."

And Tanner's cell phone rang.

"Sam, Josh, you know George Winkler of the Colorado State Police detective bureau?"

"Met him once."

"Well, he's just called us. Pulled over a guy driving a stolen car that had a trunk full of hardware. Chinese AK 47s, matter of fact. Driver claimed he'd just picked up the car to deliver it for somebody to a shop in Colorado Springs. Said he didn't look in the trunk. Also said he picked up the vehicle, a 2007, 540 BMW, at Denver International in the airport garage. The car was unlocked and the keys were left under the floor mat, he said."

"Imagine that," Tanner said.

"Exactly. When Winkler told the suspect he believed he'd boosted the car out of state and had picked up the guns for delivery, he came up with another story. Guy is twenty and scared shitless, says a fellow named Kennedy arranged for him to deliver the car for $500. Winkler thinks this kid is a regular driver for an interstate auto ring."

"Why did Winkler stop the car?"

"The kid was speeding 15 miles over the limit down I-25. Winkler ran a check and learned the car was reported stolen two days ago. The tags had been switched. So he cuffed the kid, called for back up and a warrant. That's about it. But I told Winkler that you had a line into Kennedy and probably the car theft ring. I think we should cut him in. Oh yeah, and bring Kennedy in."

Tanner began laughing and couldn't stop until he nearly choked. "This day keeps getting better and better. And don't I love it when I can anticipate orders. At this very minute I've got Mister Kennedy in handcuffs and was coming in with him."

18

Maria Pacheco held the phone tight to her ear, the voice of Manny Saurez a purr that put a warmth in her core. He was so far but felt so close. It was time for him to come from hiding, she was sure.

"I need you," she said.

"I've got a few things to wrap up in Cuidad Juarez, but I could leave soon. What are you hearing about the Tirado investigation?"

"Nothing," she said. "I think the authorities have given up on finding anyone. They cannot be concerned so much about the death of a person like Tirado. In and out of the system all the time, he had become a nuisance to them."

Manny wasn't sure. "That doesn't mean he wouldn't become more than a nuisance. Whoever ended him must have felt that way."

Maria smiled at that, "Yes, whoever."

"Anyway," Manny said, "I believe it is all right for me to return. My papers are in order for a visit. Maybe I should take you out of this."

"Perhaps so," she said. "I think that Marsh has become dangerous." She related his chasing the car and the shootout. "It is a thing he would not have done before. I believe he has started to take some product and it is making him loco."

"They always do that at some point. So let's go. You have plenty put away.

Maria hesitated before trying to justify her indecision. "I have a chance in the next few weeks to increase the worth, but I have no other distributor but Marsh. And again, I don't like taking the chances with him"

"What about Ramon?"

"I have told him to stay away from Marsh. I want to get him out of this also."

It was Manny's turn to consider. "This is what I will do. I will be back in Colorado by Saturday. I have personal business, my sister's boy has some trouble as you know. When I get back we will talk about whether to continue with Marsh and how we can settle the business with the Martinez's. It is your call whether we abandon the business and go, or stay to fight."

"Agreed," she said.

At lunchtime she was at the stove stirring her *caldo de pollo*. Ramon sat at the kitchen table enjoying the rich smell of what he knew would turn out a disappointment. How could she mess up a chicken stew?

"Are you hungry?"

"Yes mama," he said dutifully.

After he finished his bowl of stew and said it was wonderful, he began to urge her to take his friend Sam into the operation to make up for losing Rahall and Tirado. It was a conversation they'd had twice before and she was still unpersuaded.

"More and more, I am thinking we should back off soon," Maria told her son. "We have some major collections to make, and your cab driver seems willing to make some big buys, and then I think we go before it comes down around us."

Ramon was shaken. "Listen. I can run this. You and Manny should find a nice place in Mexico and enjoy the fruits of your labor you have worked very hard, mama. You have earned a quiet life."

Pacheco smiled at him and reached over and patted his cheek. She knew full well that he wouldn't last a month by himself. If nothing else she felt that without Manny and herself looking over his shoulder, Marsh would strike a new deal with the Martinez brothers and cut Ramon out.

"I have plenty for both of us," she said. "I want you to leave this behind and we will take up something new. It has become too dangerous here. But don't worry for the time being. I am giving it a month or two more. You should operate as though nothing is going to change. When you deal with your former in-laws, you be accommodating. And you stay away from Marsh, *que comprender?*"

"I understand. In the meantime, I have information about a major new buyer in the Marsh circle—a man named Jack."

Maria puckered her lips thoughtfully. "How do you know this?"

"My taxi driver Sam has told me. He said he had intelligence that Jack tried to buy fifty pounds of crystal but that it was more than Marsh had on hand. He said the man has let it be known that he will buy much more and guns too. Should I try to contact this man?"

"Absolutely not. Let Marsh deal with him. When accounting time comes, I will have that information. If the money is right we can take it from there."

"You have never met my cab driver. Do you think it is time?"

"I will let you know. Has he asked again?"

Ramon shook his head no. He said Sam had been out of the state making deliveries.

"Maybe I will meet him soon," Maria said. "But don't mention that to him if you see him."

When Ramon left, she poured herself shot of tequila and contemplated what she should do. When Suarez arrived next Saturday they would plan to the settle the Martinez account. Manny, she knew, would like nothing better.

Sherry Sanford knew that her time was ticking with Jay Ray Marsh. She could almost hear it. What she couldn't be sure of was if it would be a simple winding down, or an explosion. Marsh was becoming more demanding and rougher in bed as he dipped deeper into the meth. Jay Ray prided himself on not having a record, but Sherry worried that he now believed himself invincible. His recklessness was sure to attract attention.

Jay Ray was in Texas and hadn't called in two days. It was late and snowy outside, and now she'd built herself a little buzz with her pipe, some blow and just a few tequilas. Her iPod was cranked, Annie Lennox singing "you lit a torch in the empty night, " and Sherry decided she was lonely. Not for Jay Ray, the jerk. The thought came unexpectedly, *what about the dishy deputy just down the road? Rich? Ray? Last name Ballard?*

She fished through her purse and came up with the card he'd

given her and dialed the number. It took a few rings and he answered cautiously, not recognizing her number.

"It's Sherry," she said. There was a pause. "Sanford. The night at the diner in Fountain."

"Oh sure. Great. What's up?" His voice went warm.

"I may have something for you." She glanced at her watch, nine o'clock. "Are you on duty?"

"Just began my shift."

"Can you spare a few minutes, sometime around ten? I can meet you where we had breakfast."

"You're on," he said. "Just don't drive that race car of yours over the limit getting here. We got patrols jointly with the state boys all over the interstate tonight."

Driving it carefully took her an hour to get there and she arrived before him, taking the empty booth in the back. She smoked a cigarette and downed a diet coke by the time he got there, a half hour late. He didn't bother to apologize.

"So what's on your mind?"

"I'm working on something for you," she said, letting the words hang for a moment, then adding, "I want something in writing that says I'm your agent, immune from arrest. Is that a possibility?"

"It depends on what you're into. If you murder somebody, rob a bank, run over an old lady, no, it won't protect you. But I can give you a hand-written note stating that you're working on assignment for the department. That'll have to do."

Disappointed but in no position to argue, she dragged on her cigarette, snubbed it out in an ashtray and nodded in agreement.

"Before I write this," he said. "what are you talking about?"

"I can provide you with information about stolen cars. I hear things. The people I'm around think I'm just for a good time, booze and blowjobs. It's kept me safe. But I know that in a few weeks something is coming down."

"Good," said Ballard, taking a pen from his pocket and writing, "This is to identify Sherry Sanford, black hair, blue eyes, five feet eight inches tall and approximately 120 pounds, with a tiny scar at the corner of her mouth. She is working with the El Paso County Sheriff's Office on an undercover assignment." He signed it "Raymond W. Ballard, deputy sheriff" and pushed it across the table.

She read it, folded it and put in her purse. She sat back, stretching out her long legs and making contact with his ankle. He felt a chubby coming on.

"Can we go somewhere?" she asked. "Can you be out of your car for a while?

"Actually, I have a place three blocks away. Follow me. I'm going to call in with a tummy ache. I anticipated this might take a fun turn, so I told the lieutenant I wasn't feeling too good. How much time do you have?"

"I got all night if you're up to it."

Ballard laughed, "I'm practically up already."

She followed him to downtown Fountain where he rented a second-floor apartment in an older house at the top of a hill. He had a swank kitchen in brushed steel, a large living room with a fireplace and above that a fifty-inch flat screen TV. On an adjoining wall in a glass-front cabinet, she saw shelves of electronic gadgets. There was good art on the walls, nothing cowboy, and Sherry was impressed, guessing that he had family money or was supplementing a deputy's pay with something hinkey. Whatever, she liked what she saw of the place and when she got his pants off, him, too.

19

Two days after his introduction to Marsh, Tanner got a call from him asking for a meeting. "Let's talk some business," Marsh said. "There's a club down the street from the Antlers Hotel. How 'bout there?"

There were a couple reasons Tanner didn't want to meet him at the downtown club. The place was so noisy the wire he'd wear would be useless, and it would be hard for his backup team to get through the crowd fast if it got dicey.

"I know the place and it's always jammed. How about I meet you on the curb outside and we take a ride in my car."

"No way. We'll meet there and you follow me to a shopping center near the Interstate. Say 10 p.m.?"

Tanner agreed.

"Josh is out of town but I have to do this fast or the fish wiggles off the hook," he said. "He's eager though, just two days after we made the buy at Crowe's. He's jumped the three-day wait these guys make to see if they get arrested. But he's nervous, so tell the guys to be careful."

"We'll be invisible," Moore promised.

Tanner figured Marsh had most of his dope on the street and was waiting for the collections. Much of the drug business, especially meth, is done on a front basis because the dealers don't have big cash reserves. The drug is parceled as the distributor sells it and returns the agreed purchase price. For Ice, the best meth, that's $1,200 an ounce and nearly twenty grand for a pound lot. A dealer like Marsh would cream his jeans to get a steady upfront cash connection and not have to advance the product, and he seemed to believe he'd found one in Tanner who'd been quick to pay that way.

Tanner called Sally to say he'd be late and to put his dinner in the fridge. It was the third time in a week, and it left his chain hanging out there, so she jerked it, hard.

"You know it's three weeks to Christmas," she told him, "and I don't suppose you've had time to do any shopping." And before he could answer she added, "Of course not."

"Well . . ." he began.

"That's not necessarily a bad thing," she interrupted. "Because the girls have decided they want a pony, preferably one each, for Christmas."

"Shit," said Tanner.

"Mmm-hmm, word in the neighborhood is ponies do that. You might get a shovel, too."

"Sally, you can't be serious."

"Yes, Sam, I can't be. Unless you know where there's an extra ten grand to fence the back lot and put up a shed. But I think you might want to find time soon to sit down with the girls and do what fathers do best."

"Say no."

"Yes, say no. I'm tired of saying it and them not hearing it. It'll go better for them to be furious with you, since you're not here."

This wasn't going well at all and Tanner had to ask, "Sally, are we having a fight?"

She gave a laugh but it was a little one. "No, Sam, not really. But I'm ready for this case to get wrapped up."

"I'm wrapping and wrapping," he said, "and putting a bow on it for Christmas."

"Goodie for us," she said and hung up.

Tanner called Sammy Moore to organize the surveillance for his meeting with Marsh. He'd be watched over by six men in four cars driving the box pattern, with a vehicle tailing, one ahead, and two keeping pace on either side a block away.

It was just after 10 when Tanner pulled his "beater" behind Marsh's

BMW parked curbside at the club's entrance, and tapped the horn. Marsh looked in the rearview, caught his eye and waved for him to follow. Three miles on, Marsh turned behind a convenience store on the edge of a shopping center and stopped. As a show of faith Tanner left his car and got into Marsh's. The dealer, he noticed, was far snappier than most of his colleagues, wearing a black belted knee-length leather coat, black jeans and black suede ankle boots. His short brown hair framed a clean-shaven face dominated by a chin so large that Tanner figured it took half the morning to shave it.

They shook hands and Tanner said he had only about 30 minutes, so what did Marsh have in mind? Before he could answer, Tanner asked, "What are you carrying?

".357 magnum."

"Can I see it?"

Marsh stared at him, then pulled the weapon from his shoulder holster, opened the cylinder and let the shells empty into his free hand before passing Tanner the weapon. Tanner admired it a minute, then glanced at the shells in Marsh's palm and noticed two were birdshot.

"What's the deal with your ammo?"

Marsh got a serious look. "If I get an argument during a collection, I don't want to hurt 'em so bad they can't pay up, just scare hell out of 'em, mostly. So I use the bird shot on their legs. Also, sometimes there's a woman and children around. Don't want to clip anybody in front of their family. Ain't civilized 'cause then you got to do the family. So I load it shot, slug, shot, and the rest slugs for just in case."

They grinned at each other.

"It's real considerate of you. I'd never thought of that," Tanner said. "Might borrow the idea."

He handed the pistol back. So. What you got for me?"

Marsh unfolded a sheet of paper he pulled from a shirt pocket, looked it over and then looked at Tanner.

"How about twenty-five AK-47s, five pounds of C-4 explosives and three night vision goggles?"

Tanner stared back at him, stunned. "You can get all that?"

"Hoss, I've got all that," Marsh said, laughing.

"What you've got to be is shitting me. How? From where?"

"A Navy Seal brought it back from Iraq. He flipped it to me for a bulk order of Ice. Says he's got a way to bring in more that can't be traced. This batch, they're Iraqi army AKs, special price to you of $1,000 each. Goggles, $2,000 each. The C-4 frankly I don't know what to ask for it, never handled anything like it. Make your offer."

No question but Tanner would meet his price. This stuff had to be gotten off the street fast, and he had to get it before Marsh found other buyers. If he got it to Mexico he'd double his price.

"I'll take it all. And what about my fifty pounds of meth? The question is, are you able to give me that much?"

Marsh's chest swelled. "I'm big enough and about to get bigger. I'm the biggest distributor in the area right now and I'm going to move to another supplier."

"You're quitting the Pachecos?"

Marsh shrugged, his face was set in a sneer. He was plainly smarting under Tanner's perception that he was a second level player.

"I'm just saying. . ." A silence stretched as Marsh stared out the window, making up his mind what to say. Then he said, "I have 35 guys on the street as distributors of Ice and my organization includes both gun suppliers and six guys providing me with stolen cars, which I peddle through a guy named Kennedy, who's been a gofer for the Pachecos. Originally, they were just stripping down vehicles, turning them into load carriers to haul the ingredients to various cookers all the way to California. I got Kennedy to expand into a high-end business—Beemers and Mercs, Lexus, Caddies. I got a guy can take 'em right off the lot with keys. Get 'em to Mexico, nobody's askin' 'bout papers."

This was amazing, Tanner thought, met the guy twice and he's laying out his organization just the way Ramon Pacheco did his. They must be running full strength stupid powder in their meth.

"Yeah, get 'em to Mexico, adios," Tanner said, stretching his legs out and leaning back in the seat. "Just one worry. You have to bring them across state lines and that means feds, mainly FBI."

"She-it," Marsh laughed. "Those fuckers couldn't find their peckers if they was butt naked in a tittie bar. The worry is state cops. They're the ones out on the road all the time. But the FBI, got their heads in their paperwork, forget it."

"Got to be a risk getting through the border," Tanner said, figuring he might as well get Marsh to lay out the entire operation while he wore the wire.

"Who says anything about crossing a border. Go around it. Texas got about 400 miles of coast. All you got to do is motor south, hang a right."

Tanner shook his head in wonderment. "You got the boats to do that?"

"Naw, hoss, I'm just sayin,' how it could be done."

"What about the Coast Guard?"

"They watch shipping coming this way. Don't suppose they're thinking much 'bout what's being smuggled out. But hey, ain't really my concern. I get the vehicles, and sometimes guns, to Corpus or Port Aransas, let the beaners worry from there."

Talk died as both men spotted the CSPD patrol entering the lot and tensed as it turned toward them. The officer steered straight for Marsh's parked car.

Marsh pulled a small semi auto from his jacket pocket and put it on his lap, then began reloading the .357 he'd cleared before letting Tanner take a look at it.

"How fast can you get to your car?" he asked Tanner. "If he stops here and gets out I'm going to pop him."

"Wait a minute! Wait a minute!" Tanner reached over and put his hand over Marsh's gun. "Let me see if I can take care of this. Stay cool."

The patrolman parked with his car pointed at Marsh's vehicle, opened his door and got out. Tanner was thankful he didn't know the man. He got out of Marsh's SUV and walked around in front to greet the officer, his hands clearly visible. Marsh had his window down and could hear the conversation.

"What's the problem, officer?" Tanner said.

"Is there some reason you two are sitting back here? You're making the convenience store manager pretty nervous. He called us. He has been robbed a couple of times."

"Officer, we're two old friends who hadn't seen each other for some time. We met at a stoplight down the street and pulled over to chat a few minutes. I certainly can understand the manager's concerns but you can assure him we're law abiding citizens who have no intention of doing anything illegal. We pulled back here to keep out of the way of the holiday mall traffic."

The patrolman thought a moment, studying the big man in front of him and the man in the car. Just as he was about to ask for identification, his car radio crackled and a dispatcher called out "car alpha-one-five, officer needs assistance, 3229 Monroe Street. Where are you?"

"I don't have time for this," the patrolman said, "but you guys need to go have your chat somewhere else. That store manager is spooked."

"That was close," Marsh said, as Tanner walked back to the car.

Tanner thought, no, you clown, not unless you made it close. He didn't get back into Marsh's SUV but leaned on the driver's side door. "Listen, don't cowboy up when I'm in a car. This was easy. But the last thing I want to be involved in is a hit on a police officer. Mugs I could care less about, but cops are a different. Understood?"

"Okay," the Texan said, grudgingly. 'It's just I have this thing about jail, never been, never going."

"All right. I think we've settled some things. Going to take me a couple days put together the cash for that weaponry. You get that load of meth together, let me know when and I'll take that off your hands, too."

They shook hands through the window and Tanner headed for his car. Sweat was running down his neck into in his collar. How close was that? Had the cop gotten down to the driver's license business it could have gone really bad. He was glad his surveillance team was on the ball.

"I don't know who provided the officer needs assistance call," he said into his wire. "But thanks."

He sat in his car until Marsh pulled out ahead of him, then drove to the front of the convenience store and went in. A few minutes later he was out again with a container of coffee, smiling as the manager waved at him. Marsh, who had pulled over at the far end of the lot to watch, nodded to himself and waited until Tanner's big Buick rolled out toward the Interstate. That was smooth, he thought, this dude is going to be an asset. He picked up his cell and dialed Sherry.

"Meet me at the club," he said when she answered.

Tanner meantime was making a wide circle before heading downtown toward his office. He knew at least one of the watchers would trail Marsh to make certain he didn't follow Tanner. The predicted snow was beginning to come down steadily and Tanner decided to stay the night on his office couch, too tired for the long drive home to the wife and daughters who were already peeved about his absence.

20

Tanner opened the office refrigerator to get three bottles of beer he'd been saving, while Mike Reach and Sammy Moore unwrapped take-out sandwiches on the ATF conference table.

Moore took a bite of his burger and a swig of Buffalo Gold, then sat back and looked at Tanner. "Gutsy performance out there, m'man. This guy Marsh has got to be a user. He's twitchy as a whore with hives, thought he was sure going to pop the cop."

"Oh, he was," said Tanner. "If I hadn't intercepted the officer before he got to the car, it was heading south fast. I'd have whacked Marsh first, but then you know the cop would have fired on me!"

Moore finished a bite of ham and swiss before answering, "The guy is something else, but he's cagey. We haven't found any property around here in his name. Before I got here the surveillance team radioed in that he'd gone to that club where you met him. They're going to stay with him until he leaves to find out where the fucker lives."

Tanner took a last pull on his beer, balled up his sandwich wrapping and lobbed it into a wastebasket in the far corner, three points. He looked out the window at a furious snowfall blowing sideways. "It's rough out there," he said. "I wouldn't want to be out in that, bird dogging that dude. Maybe you ought to call the rest off. We'll find out his location later."

Moore considered the snow and had to agree. He dialed Rush who was leading the surveillance, "Call it off and get the hell home." Turning back to Tanner, he said, "So. Our next move?"

Tanner said Marsh was to get back to him in a few days, giving him time to pull together money for the AK-47s and the C-4. "Getting that load out of his hands and off the streets is top priority. Gadsden is focused on Ft. Carson, tracking the Navy Seal."

"We know who it is?"

"We've identified two Seals presently there," Tanner said. "One drove in from San Diego pulling a U-Haul he rented there. It's still parked in a secure lot near the base. We're watching it."

"What's a Seal doing at an Army base?" Reach wondered.

"Some kind of inter-service course they're taking, or maybe teaching, I'm not clear which," Tanner explained. "Both Seals are master chiefs."

"And we're not rolling them up because. . .?"

"We do that now and Marsh could get wind of it, dump the weapons and explosives. We want it in our hands, then we can grab the rogue Seal. Whichever one it is, he's going nowhere. We've got eyes on both, round the clock. Gadsden's in charge of that detail."

Reach had been detached on assignment in Denver for much of the past week and felt he'd slipped out of the loop. "It's moving so fast in so many different directions, I'm kind of lost. Where do I fit."

"Glad you asked," Tanner said. "How about you liaise with the Colorado State Police on the car theft angle? That one's really their baby and you've got the best contacts with CSP. If we get some money changing hands in Kennedy's front room, we might have the Martinez brothers in a vise."

Reach looked puzzled. "Explain that one to me. Last I heard, you were putting JoJo Kennedy back in the joint for some hard time. He's out already?"

Moore and Tanner looked at each other and laughed. Moore said, "Our man Sam here plays dirty. Legal, but dirty. Tell him, Sam."

Tanner pointed to the hallway. "I marched his fat ass down there to the holding pen. Told him I was keeping him there overnight because by the time I got paperwork done it would be too late to drive him to the Cripple Creek Jail. And that's where he'd stay, Cripple Creek, for his own safety of course."

"Ooo," said Reach, "that's mean."

The Cripple Creek Jail was arguably the worst in West and notorious among the legally challenged. It was built in the 1880s on the third floor of a mercantile building. Its cell is a six-by-nine-foot box, constructed of half-inch steel plates held together with steam engine rivets. It smells like a hundred and thirty years of urine and rust and for light there is one bare, dim bulb. The only upside was, since a cell held only one at a time, you wouldn't get buggered. Of course, depending on your predilection, that could be another downside. The steel box was very familiar to Kennedy because that's where the State Police placed him after his latest bust.

"He really, really didn't want to go there again, for some reason," Tanner said. "Actually, our pen didn't seem to agree with him, either."

The ATF holding cell at the farthest end of the suite was a four-by-nine cinder-block room with no outside window and a stainless steel toilet-sink combo behind a solid metal door. It is the common design of all modern prison. Kennedy, however, was not of sufficient fiber himself for modern prison life and quickly knew it.

"I thought he was going to have the DTs before I let him go," Tanner said. "If that joker doesn't get a drink on the hour, he's got serious shakes."

"He didn't try to lawyer up?"

"Hell, I Mirandized him, told him I'd let him call every lawyer in the phonebook. He didn't want one. He's our friend now, he'll do anything to stay where he's never more than sixty minutes from his next drink."

"So he's our lead to Marsh and maybe the Martinezes."

"Yeah, but keep the lead short and be quick to give the choke-chain a jerk."

When Reach and Moore left, Tanner went back to his office and stood at the window. It was coming down too hard to think about making it home or even slogging the two blocks down the street to the hotel, and he'd crash on his couch while Colorado buried itself under a foot of snow. He went to his closet for the blanket his wife called the Other Woman, lay down and wrapped into it and slept soundly.

Maria Pacheco's shaky world turned upside down in one interrupted phone call. She was awakened from a dream of white clouds and white beaches by the ringing at 2 a.m. She fumbled the phone to her ear and heard the voice of her cousin Dominga, sobbing. It went on for several minutes and then the connection broke before she could reply.

She sat up, not believing what was happening. She understood it was true but couldn't accept belief of it. The one person in the world she could count on was gone, and there was no consolation in the fact it was not of his choosing. She sat unmoving for ten minutes before numbly punching in her son's number. It rang five times and just before his recorded leave a message Ramon answered, "What the fuck?"

"Get over here."

It took him half an hour to get dressed, promise the woman in his bed he'd be back for breakfast and drive the mile to his mother's house. He found her still sitting on the edge of bed in her nightgown, hugging herself tightly. There were no tears. She had lost two husbands but the grief was nothing to what she now felt. God was punishing her. She had skipped confession, she had not supported her religion, she had ordered people killed. This was His retribution for her sins.

Suddenly she wailed her pain. Ramon sat and put his arms around her. Now he could guess what it was, "Manny?"

His shirt was wet before she could quit sobbing against her son's chest to choke out, Dead."

It was almost dawn before she could stop crying and lay quiet enough for Ramon to make some calls to Juarez. He was told that Manny had stepped into a squabble between his sister's youngest son and a manager in *La Familia* cartel. There had been some negotiations and things seemed to be settled. Manny was leaving his sister's house with suitcase in hand to get into a cab to the airport when a fusillade of bullets shredded him. Gunmen who'd been waiting in two parked vans then ran into the house and shot Manny's sister, her son, his wife, their five small children and stomped their two little dogs to death before driving off, hooting and laughing.

Ramon called a doctor they used in emergencies to come give Maria a sedative that knocked her out until mid-afternoon. When she could raise up, Ramon brought her a small carafe of coffee to jolt her awake. She sipped it and stared out the window next to her bed, eyes hurting from the glare outside from the snowfall of the night before. She shivered, put down the cup and pulled the covers up to her chin, feeling as if she'd never be warm again.

"We need to talk, Mama," Ramon said. " If you feel up to it."

She nodded and said in a voice hoarse from grief, "With Manny gone I have lost my will to continue. We must plan how we can get out of the arrangements we are in. Or I can transfer my responsibilities to you. I want nothing more to do with this."

"Please, Mama, give yourself some time," Ramon pleaded. "My brothers and sisters live comfortably in Mexico on what you provide. We need you strong."

Maria leaned back in her bed and closed her eyes. She patted his hand as she settled back under the covers again. Ramon asked if she would want to go to Mexico for a service.

"I think not," she muttered and was asleep.

21

Kennedy claimed he directed the activities of eight car thieves boosting vehicles in Colorado and Kansas. To build a comprehensive case on the hot-car operation, the investigators wanted evidence tying the boosters to buyers. Tanner and state police detective George Winklers would pose as the buyers, and the deals would go down in Kennedy's living room, where they'd be recorded and videoed. An agency tech team called down from Denver entered the house at midnight on Sunday and had the cameras and audio pickups in place before sunup.

Tanner saw them out, clapped a hand on the flabby shoulder of his new informant and said, "JoJo, think you can get a few of your sellers over this evening for some fun and profit?"

"Uh, maybe," Kennedy said.

"No, no, you're sure. Whatever it takes, have them here by eight or I'll have you in the Cripple Creek cooler by nine. I'll be Jack and my partner will be George. We'll take what they have available, cash on the spot."

Kennedy muttered agreement.

At 8 p.m. Tanner and Winklers sat in the old Buick with the new V-8 engine half a block down from Kennedy's ramshackle rambler. Both were wired. Winkler had a briefcase with $20,000 in state money. At 8:15 two pickup trucks pulled up in front of the house and two men in their twenties got out and walked to the door. Both were thin and pale, wearing baseball caps, jeans, work boots and down vests.

The officers waited fifteen minutes to let them get settled and to see if anyone else showed, before walking into the house without knocking, startling Kennedy who was pouring bourbon into a tall glass.

"Jesus . . .," he said, about to protest but falling silent at the look from Tanner. He introduced the young men as Mike and Bud, who could have been twins except for Bud's crop of pimples and Mike's array of ear studs. Neither made eye contact or said hello.

"Let's do business," said Tanner. "What do you have?"

Bud handed Kennedy a list -- a 2007 Toyota Celica; a 2009 Nissan Murano crossover, a 2002 BMW 540 with 55,000 miles and a 2008 Chevrolet Impala, all allegedly with low mileage, and Kennedy passed it to Tanner.

"How much for the lot?"

"All for $30,000 and that's a bargain," Kennedy said. "The BMW is worth $15,000 and the Murano is Blue Book at $24K. The whole package ought to bring fifty-K, but we want to do more business so we'll settle for that."

Winkler stepped in. "I don't think we want the Beemer, Jack. Too easy to spot. And the Toyota's a dog. Let's take the other two. Say $20,000?"

Kennedy showed disappointment -- and Tanner wondered if he actually thought he'd get to keep the money -- but bobbed his head in agreement.

"Where are the cars?" Tanner asked.

Bud said, "The Murano's in public parking at Patty Jewett golf course and the Impala is at the lot at Memorial Park." He put the keys on the coffee table.

Winkler took the keys and went to make sure the vehicles were where Bud claimed. To make conversation while waiting for Winkler to call in, Tanner asked how Bud had snagged the Murano.

He sniggered. "Cold mornings, me and Mike drive around neighborhoods, looking for cars sitting in driveways, warming up. 'Bout half the time the owner's gone back in his house to wait for it. Mike ran up and got the Murano that way yesterday."

Mike looked proud and Tanner laughed along with them.

"The Impala?"

Bud said, "Kind of the same way. We were sitting at a 7/11 on Platte, guy pulls up, leaves his engine running while he goes inside, Mike was behind the wheel before the door closed behind that asshole."

Mike still said nothing but smiled and stared at the floor, pleased at the acknowledgment of his skills.

Tanner shook his head and agreed there sure were a lot of assholes leaving keys in their cars. He knew another common car theft was to get a source working at a dealership who could lift a spare set of keys to a vehicle. A booster could drive it right off the lot or, so not to burn the inside guy, wait for the car to be sold, then wait a little longer and go to the buyer's home some night and take it.

"Got anybody inside at a dealer?" It would be another thief for CSP to round up when it was time to arrest Bud and Mike.

Both young men looked unhappy at the question. "Did 'til last month," Bud said. "Guy I went to high school with was working at Friendly Auto Sales. Passed us keys to two sweet ones. But then, some cop came around asking questions of the manager and Hank spooked. Quit, and I don't know where he went."

"Tough," said Tanner, knowing it would be easy for CSP to track down the Hank who'd recently worked for Friendly Auto.

"Yeah," said Bud. "Uh, you know anybody with a dealer?"

"Maybe. I'll give it some thought," said Tanner.

About 9:30 his cell rang and Winkler reported he found both stolen cars hidden where Bud had said   . Tanner put the briefcase on the table and dumped out the cash.

He stood and gave the three thieves a friendly smile. "Be seein' you."

22

John Tremain had been a dealer for Marsh for about two months. That's all it took for his neighbors in Cragmor Heights to get suspicious of so many people coming at all hours to his old bungalow in the middle of the block. No one seemed to stay long and that suggested something odd happening there. Louie Smithson was a retired civilian employee of the North American Air Defense Command who had lived for 36 years in the house across the street from that weird looking young man. He knew Sergeant Taylor Rush of the CSPD because his son had played summer league ball with him, so he gave him a call.

"I think they're dealing drugs." Smith told the officer.

Rush agreed to check it out and get back to him. He really doubted that anyone would be selling drugs out of his house in this old neighborhood, home to so many old military types putting around their properties all day long. Only an idiot could think to get away with it in view of all the geezers trained their entire careers to be wary of perimeters. But, he'd find a couple hours to watch the place.

Two nights later he parked his unmarked car in Smithson's driveway and leaned back, thinking he was in for a boring evening and would have trouble keeping awake. What he saw was an eye-opener, car after car pulling up to the house and men and women of apparently wide range of social status entering the house, coming out after a few minutes and speeding away. Rush watched for an hour and saw twenty cars come and go.

Something hinkey was happening in there and the sergeant decided to check priors on the occupant of record, to see if he could find probable cause for a search warrant. John Tremain turned out to be a

28-year-old ex-Army enlisted man from Ohio who had left the service six months earlier. He had a juvenile record for drug possession but had not been arrested since. His discharge from the service was general, not honorable, indicating some kind of behavior the army wouldn't tolerate. It wasn't enough for a search right away but it begged for a stakeout.

For three nights Rush and his backup watched the house and saw no action at all. The officers figured that somehow Tremain had been tipped off but would later learn he'd only sold out his meth supply. On the fourth night cars began arriving in front of the residence and the surveillance team saw half a dozen men going in – but in contrast to previous nights, they didn't come right back out.

The sergeant radioed for backup from a SWAT unit and they hit Tremain's house at 10:15 – to find half a dozen men scrambling to hide drugs and guns. A tall man in a shiny suit and no tie stood up and demanded to see their warrant.

"If there are drugs and guns here," he said, "I did not know that. I certainly don't have any."

"Oh yeah?" Rush countered. "Why in hell are you wearing a shoulder holster? Keep condoms in it? Toothbrush?"

Jay Ray Marsh had managed to slip his .357 under a cushion on the opposite couch when police began banging on the door but hadn't time to shuck the holster. Nobody had even a minute to dump the twenty-five pounds of methamphetamine, either.

What the CSPD had interrupted was a meeting to allocate and package the latest meth shipment. Marsh had no idea that his man Tremain had been selling to tweakers directly from the house, which was a designated drop-and-share shop. Now, for the first time in his life, Marsh was being busted and he could kill somebody.

"How in the fuck did this meeting get out?" he whispered to Tremain. "There has to be a leak."

Marsh and his crew were booked on drug and weapons charges and brought before a magistrate within hours. The assistant prosecutor asked for $100,000 bond on each count. But because Marsh himself had no priors his lawyer got his bond dropped to $50,000. It was a break, but while Marsh could easily cover ten percent he have to prove he had collateral to cover the balance. He'd have to pledge a rental house he had put in Sherry Sanford's name. Although he also had the penthouse condominium in the Springs, he didn't want that touched. It would take him four or five days to get everything arranged through Roy Crowe, who had been late coming to the meeting and watched from afar as it went down.

When he could Crowe visited his boss and found him still furious.

"How'd this happen?" Marsh demanded.

"I haven't the slightest, Jay Ray."

"I still think there's a rat inside. How come you weren't there?"

The implication was clear.

"Woah," Crowe protested. "You can't make me for this. I was fifteen minutes late because of traffic and I was driving right into the thing. Man, I hate you for thinking I'd do something like that."

"Okay, Okay," Marsh said, but there was something in his voice that left Crowe uneasy.

Marsh made bond in three days and went straight to Sherry's apartment where he holed up, trusting nobody but her, and her not much. He placed calls down his chain of command, trying to get a sense of who might be a snitch, and spent most of the day listening to people who were quick to point suspicion at their best friends. What he got from it was the clearest picture that his closest associates were untrustworthy, and while it didn't pinpoint an informant, it did make him more paranoid. He took some toot, which made him more so.

In late afternoon he turned on the TV and was immediately intrigued by the picture of a young man hunched low over a speeding motorcycle being followed by news helicopters and flashing blue lights down I-25. The guy on the chopper looked familiar. Marsh leaned forward and studied the rider as the TV camera gave a closer-up view, and he recognized the leathers, the screaming eagle embossed on the back of the red and black jacket, the Nazi-style helmet. He could tell by the build and the body motions, *Fuck, it's Bud*.

Tanner was in his office, shuffling papers into end-of-day piles when he answered the phone on his desk to hear CSP's George Winkler say, "Quick, turn on Channel 13. You aren't going to believe this. . ."

Tanner clicked the remote and got an overhead view of a motorcycle being chased by patrol cars of the El Paso County Sheriff's Department.

"Recognize that guy on the cycle?" Winkler asked.

"Uh, no, should I? All I can see right now on this little screen is some dude's rear end. Of course, I recognize that's a sight more familiar to state police."

"Watch it, asshole. That's one of the thieves working for Kennedy. In fact, according to the tags on the bike, he's the guy who gave us that stolen car list."

"Holy shit. I'll call you back." Tanner ran down the hall to Groton's office. "You've got to see this. "Turn your tube. One of the guys working for Kennedy and Marsh, he's in full flight."

The two agents stared at the set as the motorcycle zoomed around the traffic, followed by three sheriff's cars, lights flashing, sirens wailing. It was a masterful ride, swooping between cars on the Interstate going north toward Denver. At one point, a deputy's cars got within maybe thirty yards of the biker but had to drop back to avoid a slow moving sedan.

Tanner's cell phone went off. It was Marsh and he walked into the hall to take it.

"Where are you?"

"Conducting some business," Tanner said.

"If you're near a television, switch it on to channel 13. There's a goddamn chase going on you won't believe."

Tanner walked back into Groton's office to let the announcer's voice filter through to Marsh.

"Yeah, so what?"

"That's one of my guys," said Marsh.

"You sure?"

"Sure, I'm sure. Guy boosts vehicles, makes some sales for me. If he gets away, can you help?"

"Don't know about that. What you got in mind?"

"He's going to need some cash, which I don't have right now after making bail. I want him to get the hell out of town."

It was a strange request, even from somebody who seemed to need to be his new best friend, and Tanner tried to make some sense of it. "This's a car booster, Jay Ray, what could a guy like that be to you?"

Marsh's sigh came strong over the phone. "He used to work for me at, uh, where I worked before, and then we got into, uh, doing this and I started going up and he kinda went sideways. So, y'know, we go back. I don't hang with him but, uh, I got to look out for him."

There were enough uh's there to suggest Marsh was struggling to understand himself, but Tanner could see no downside to appear to be helping.

"Alright. It doesn't look like he's got a chance of out-running these guys," Tanner said, "but if he does, count on me," and hung up.

Tanner went back to his desk and called home to say he'd be on the way by five. The girls had colds and were acting up, Tinker the cat was missing in action, Alpo the chowhound had gas something wicked, the furnace kept shutting off, the wind kept rattling that loose shutter at the upstairs hall window, and Sally's mood had sunk to the occasion.

By the time he got off the phone, sour now himself and in no hurry to scoot homeward, the motorcycle rider had turned off the Interstate into the high country, two patrol cars in pursuit had spun out of control and into each other, and the TV news helicopter had lost site of the fugitive. Now the station flashed a picture of the suspect and his identification -- Howard Wilson, 25, of Denver, known to Tanner as the thief called Bud.

He was clicking off the lights before heading home an hour later when Marsh called back, elated. "He got away. You believe that? He went into a slide at sixty miles an hour and stopped at the edge of a ravine near Monument and he took off running. The cops lost him."

"Know where he is?" Tanner asked and immediately answered himself, "Dumb question. Of course you do."

"He's at the Garden of Gods Motel 8, room 317."

"Okay, I'll send George over with cash and clothes. He'll give him a quick ride to Pueblo where he can catch a bus. They won't be looking for him that far south so quickly. Your man knows George. He was with me when we made the buys from Kennedy. Tell him it will take 30 to 45 minutes and not to get nervous and stay inside. Is he armed?"

"Don't think so," Marsh said. "He always says, last thing he wants is a gunfight."

Tanner called Winkler and told him that he had located the fugitive and where to find him.

"You got that done, sitting in your office?" Winkler was incredulous.

"Told you I was good," Tanner laughed. "Here's what you do. Call the CSPD fugitive squad and tell them where to find this guy but only after you get there yourself. Wait until you see the cops arrive and then as they're ushering Wilson out the door, you drive slowly by. Let him get a look at you."

Winkler was watching when the cops arrived As they led the biker out of his room, he stopped his car to rubberneck as any commuter would. Wilson looked up, recognized him and shook his head, warning him off.

Winkler called Tanner who dialed Marsh.

"Winkler says he got there just as the cops did and watched him get dumped in a patrol car. It's just luck, the cops didn't make my man. Who else did Wilson call besides you? Your bunch is leaking like a sieve."

Marsh was furious, but not at him. He was sure now there was a leak in his organization somewhere.

"Thanks for the help, Jack. I'll call soon."

At the time, he didn't know how soon.

Just two days after Wilson's arrest, Marsh called to say he needed to get another crew member out of town. "I got a man with multiple warrants on him. Can you give him the same support?"

"I think I can do that," Tanner said, keeping the laugh out of his voice. "Where is he?"

"Same place, Motel 8, room 522"

"You always put your guys there?"

"It's easy access in and out, on the interstate, and the owner likes product, he owes me."

"All right," Tanner said. "Give him the same instructions. I'd go myself this time but I'm tied up. George will pick him up and bring him to me." He paused and said, "I hope nothing goes wrong this time, Jay Ray. If it does, you better find your rat somewhere."

Three hours later Tanner called Marsh, shouting into the phone, "George just called. He got there and was walking to the room when he saw cops turning in off the street, had to run for it. Fuck's sake, man, I'm not putting my guys at risk like this anymore. George got back to his car okay, sat there and watched the fuzz drag your guy away."

Tanner began to laugh so hard when he got off the phone that Groton came to his door to join in the joke. "What the hell's up? We can hear you all the way down the hall."

When he explained the situation, Groton was disbelieving.

"Every time he turns to you, his man goes down and he can't figure it out."

"No but don't ask me why. For some reason I've become his best friend."

They were mulling Marsh's gullibility when Winkler rang and reported that their latest fugitive Walter Anderson, 38, of Wichita, had been processed and wasn't likely to go free again before the Rockies eroded flat.

"The locals can't believe you," Winkler said. "You've given 'em two collars in three days and taken no credit for yourself. The head of the fugitive squad is telling folks that if you'd been FBI and not ATF they'd of fired you for that kind of cooperation."

"You told them I was the tip?"

"Hell yes. You guys have been outstanding through this whole thing. Sort of restores their faith in how things are supposed to work."

23

"Marsh has shut everything down," Tanner reported at the Monday morning staff meeting. "The deal with the C-4 and AK's is on hold. He's not supplying meth to his distributors. It's a full stop."

Tanner explained that the arrest of Marsh's top car thieves, and what he believed was their betrayal from the inside, had the dealer's drug-fueled paranoia revved to redline.

"He's telling me he can't trust any of his people until he finds the snitch. That means pressure up and down the line. His players aren't going to be happy about this. The fact this comes over Christmas holidays probably lets him have some slack, but the cookers and users going to be screaming soon enough."

Groton looked around the room. "Somebody give me something. Where's a pressure point?"

"The cars are key to this," Moore offered. "Without the load vehicles they have to find another way to ship the ephedrine west. Up to now they've avoided trucks because they're easier to spot and harder get rid of. But a car they can hide in any junkyard after a run or two. Maybe we should take them down now."

Groton frowned and shook off the notion. "A couple things missing. Including catching the Martinez brothers with the goods. We've followed this all the way to them but haven't got them physically involved. Just the allegations." The RAC yawned, scratched and stood up, signaling the end of the meeting. "Guess all we can do at the moment is wait and watch. Maybe one of you guys can think of a way to give 'em a goose for Christmas."

Tanner went to his government green office, shut the door and dialed up Roy Crowe on his cell. He got him on the third try. Crowe was agitated, complaining he was wasn't meeting demand for meth, saw none in sight and hadn't been able to contact Marsh for two days.

"He's shacked up with a new broad," Crowe said. "A looker but lowdown. Sherry's probably spittin' fire."

"Sherry?"

"Sherry Sandford. She's been his main for a couple years. Onetime escort girl and something else to look at. She drives that Viper you must have seen parked in the driveway the night you first came over and met Jay Ray. She was in the other room with him, helping with distribution."

"So who's the new one?"

"Don't know. Don't think she's that important. But I do know nothing's happening until Jay Ray gets tired of her and comes out of his cave. Man, this is all so fucked up."

As soon as Tanner disconnected his cell rang. Caller ID said it was DEA. It was Moore inviting him to lunch, and he had as many complaints as Crowe.

"You know you're old when you start hating Christmas," Moore said. He was divorced, his ex and his kids living in Memphis, his last posting, and his girlfriend was packing to spend Christmas with her sister in Seattle. Moore was junior in his office and stuck there through New Year's. "The music makes me want to empty my piece into the speakers. Every time I see one of those baggy-assed Santas I wanta cuff him for being a perv probably." When they sat down in a booth at the corner sandwich shop, cutesy named Della's Delly, Moore grumped, "And I'm sick of the fucking turkey. If the waitress asks me if I want turkey sandwich, I'm going to punch her."

When the waitress came they both ordered onion soup and Rubens.

"Will that be corned beef or turkey?" she smiled, and Tanner burst out laughing.

"Hear anything interesting?" Moore asked after she had left.

"Yeah. Crowe tells me Marsh is laying low, shacking with a new chic. Ramon says his mother has become a recluse since some friend of hers died in Mexico. What about the Martinez brothers?"

"Quiet. Ernesto appears to have gone back to Mexico for a holiday and Miguel is around but not doing business. No one has seen Emilio. If this is frustrating for us, you got to figure with them it's about to blow."

Crowe was right about Sherry. She was fuming when she came knocking on his door that night while he and Brenda were cozyed up on the couch watching a cage-fighting rerun. Crowe had his money on the fighter with the most tatoos, because he'd already seen the bout, but a look at Sherry told him she was more dangerous.

When the bout ended, Crowe shut off the set and fixed Sherry a vodka on the rocks and bourbon and sodas for Brenda and himself. Handing her the drink he said, "You look stressed, babe, what's the matter," knowing full well what was on her mind.

"That Texas-sized asshole," she said, lighting a cigarette and blowing the smoke at the ceiling. "I can't get Jay Ray to answer the phone and when I went by the apartment he wouldn't answer the door. And I know he was there."

"Probably screwing that skank," Brenda offered helpfully.

"You got that right. Why would he mess around with someone like that? I'm insulted." She stubbed out her cigarette and immediately reached for another.

Crowe reached over and took it out of her hand. "Jesus, Sherry the air in this place is polluted enough."

"Sorry," she said. "I'm all strung out over this. I gave up the Ice when it started making me do crazy things." She gave Crowe a look and he averted his eyes, fearing Brenda might pick up on her allusion to a threesome with Marsh.

Crowe said, "Look, I'm as concerned as you. My cash is thin and I have a lot of obligations. Users don't take holidays and we need to get back to business. But he's convinced there's a rat in the house and he's not making a move. I know this much, if he doesn't shake out of it pretty soon, either the Martinez brothers or Ramon Pacheco's going to be canceling their connection with us, and if I know them they'll try to cancel Marsh, too, while they're at it."

"What can we do?"

"I don't know. I'm having trouble talking with him too. I think I'm on his list of possible snitches even after all our time together. Only guy's getting through to him is Jack from Kansas, who he's known about a month. You believe that? "

"Can't you try to talk to him in my behalf?"

"Sure, but I'm telling you, I haven't been getting through to him myself. I don't know what good I'll do you when I do get through." He sat back on the bar stool and took a big swallow of bourbon. "I'll do that for you, Sherry. Meantime, do you have any spare cash you can lend me?

"I have about four grand I was going to put in my safety deposit box. It's in my purse." She looked around for it. "Shit, I must have left it in the car. I was so pissed about Jay Ray. It's in the front seat. The money's in an envelope in the purse."

"I'll get it" Crowe said and went outside to the Viper. The purse was sitting on the passenger seat. He opened it and pulled out a thick envelope, and as he did a small tightly folded piece of paper fell out. He started to put it back into the purse but curiosity got the best of him and he opened it.

It was Sherry Sandford's agreement with Deputy Ray Ballard to act as an informant for the El Paso County Sheriff's office. He couldn't believe his eyes. "The fucking bitch," he said aloud.

Crowe didn't know she'd never ratted on Marsh or that she'd been avoiding the deputy since spending the night with him, after getting him to sign the paper. In her mind the agreement went one way, her way, to be pulled out only if she got busted.

Crowe slipped the paper in his shirt pocket and walked back into the house and down to where the girls were bitching about that two-timing Jay Ray Marsh.

"Thanks for the money, Sherry. This'll make a difference for a week or so until I can get things loosened up and pay you back. You're a good friend. I've got an idea," he said. "I'm going to call Marsh and make a pitch for him to see you. I'll remind him how important you are to the operation. That's something he's not thinking on. How's that?"

"That would be super," she said, giving him a hug. "I'll call you later to see if things are all right before I try to call him again. I have to do some Christmas shopping."

When she was gone, Crowe went into his bedroom and closed the door and dialed Marsh's cell, practically praying he would answer.

It rang eight times before Marsh picked up, "What?"

"I know who the snitch is, I can prove it."

There was a long pause. Marsh said, "Who?"

"Sherry. Your fucking girlfriend."

"Bullshit," Marsh said, "She doesn't know all that much."

"Well she knows enough. You think she's one of your stupid bimbos, think again, pal. I'm looking at an agreement she signed with the El Paso County Sheriff's Department." He explained about it falling from her purse.

Marsh was stunned. His pride hurt but he told himself his instincts were true in cutting off everyone until he found the rat.

"I'll drop off the agreement right away if you want. Then I'll call her and say you want to make up. She'll jump at the chance."

"Do it," Marsh said. "I had a feeling about her," not considering he'd had the feeling about everybody close to him. "That's why I cut her out, that bitch, that pluperfect no good bitch." He turned to someone and said, "We're going to have some fun tonight."

"Who was that?" Crowe asked.

"Just Anna, my new squeeze. I'll be waiting."

Crowe dropped Sherry's agreement off before midnight. He didn't get her to answer her phone until the next day. She said she was tied up with relatives until the Tuesday after Christmas. He told her to go ahead and call Marsh.

Five minutes later she did. His voice was warm and he sounded disappointed she wasn't immediately free. They made plans to spend the entire New Year's weekend together.

"I'll see you then, love," she said and hung up. She had a good feeling about it.

24

New Year's Eve dawned cold and windy. There was a chance of an ice storm in the foothills and up to five inches of new base on the lower slopes, more on the expert runs higher up. Flakes fell fast by noon.

Sam and Sally Tanner once again decided to go nowhere, a tradition they had followed since they were first married. It was their time to crack a bottle of Veuve Clicquot brut and get bubbly in bed. They'd never made it to midnight yet.

Sally turned down several invitations, explaining, "Sam and I get so little time alone together." As it happened, her mother was visiting, which sent the Tanners under the covers sooner than usual. They were asleep, smiling, long before midnight.

By eight that evening in Colorado Springs, Marsh already had been hitting the Crystal, and his new friend, Anna was coking up. He could hardly wait until Sherry called. It was going to be a long night. Anna had no idea how he planned for it to end. She was in it for the fun and games. Turning on the television in the front room, he brushed off Anna's efforts to get something started. "Not yet," he told her, "company's coming."

At 11 p.m. with the snow still falling and the road slick with black ice, Fremont County Deputy Wilber Jones was cursing the weather and the fact he was stuck on patrol for two more hours. Jones was 25 and had majored in criminal justice at Colorado State. The deputy's job was just a step he hoped toward bigger things in law enforcement, if his social life could take it. His long disjointed hours and those of his college sweetheart now working as a nurse meant they rarely had romantic time together, never mind this long and so-far boring night. He was swallowing yawns now and by the time he got home he figured he'd be too tired for anything more than snoring.

Jones had pulled out of Canon City and headed north on State Road 9 toward the county line. Traffic was light and the weather sucked, and with luck he wouldn't come across any drunks before he got off duty. About three miles up, his lights picked up the taillights of a truck that seemed to be off the right side of the road. As he slowed the patrol car, he could see that it was Ryder rental truck, a two-tonner that looked to have fishtailed on some ice. The back right wheel was in the ditch.

He turned on his flashers and pulled nose-in behind the truck, phoned in his location and the license number of the vehicle, grabbed his flashlight and stepped out of his car. He approached the driver's side where a dark middle-aged man was gunning the engine, trying for traction. The deputy pointed his light at the driver and then over to where a passenger was sitting quietly, making no move to get out of the vehicle. The driver rolled down the window.

"Turn off the engine a minute," the deputy said. "Let it cool while I see how deep you're in the ditch." The driver complied.

Jones went to the back and shined his light on the wheels, dug deep in icy mud. The truck's load was too heavy and that the driver had been too impatient. It was going nowhere without a tow He walked back to the front.

"What are you hauling?" he said to the driver, who looked Hispanic. Jones noted that the passenger, somewhat younger and also Hispanic was rigidly still.

"Furniture," the driver said.

"Well, maybe we could off load some of it and lighten things up a bit. Otherwise, I'm going to have to call for a tow truck and on this night you're going to be here awhile." He paused for a moment. "May I please see your license and rental agreement?"

The driver fished his license from his wallet and the rental slip from the visor. The officer flashed his light on them and said casually, "Everything looks in order Mr. Martinez. But I need to verify that there aren't any outstanding wants or warrants. Just routine. I hope you understand. Just sit tight and I'll be right back and we can figure this out." He turned and walked toward the patrol car.

As he turned to open the door, he saw a shadow cross the road. The driver Martinez was out and headed to the opposite side. The passenger was out now too.

"Stay in the truck," Jones yelled.

He saw something in the passenger's hand and he swung the patrol car door open and ducked behind it, freeing his pistol at the same time as the door's window exploded. Another bullet from the other side of the road hit the door stanchion and burred off into the dark. Jones snapped a shot at the driver, then another at the passenger who was standing upright with both hands cupping a pistol. The deputy's bullet smacked into the passenger's torso and threw him back. Jones turned to see about the other shooter and felt something sting his ear.

"Drop your weapon," he yelled at the driver knowing it was a futile order. Martinez ran across a bare stretch of ground toward a hillock, and Jones fired twice. He grabbed for the car's radio and called for backup.

"Unit 27 officer needs assistance, shots fired three miles north on State 9, two suspects armed," he shouted, words tumbling one after another. "One man down and another fleeing on foot. I need an ambulance at this location."

The deputy pulled his shotgun out of its clamps and moved cautiously toward the man on the ground. He could feel blood trickling down his neck from where a slug nicked his ear. A centimeter to the left and he would have been on the ground, too. The passenger of the truck was trying desperately to raise himself, pushing his arms futilely on the earth, his shirtfront soaked in blood. He was muttering in Spanish, and Jones realized he was praying. The bullet had entered the left part of the man's chest, probably nicked the heart or an artery. Jones figured he was dying.

Bending down, he told the man, "Take it easy," but saw his eyes were glazing. He kicked the man's pistol out of reach and looked for the driver. Jones headed across the road, turning on the flashlight mounted under the shotgun, following footprints in the snow. There were splotches of blood and he could see that twice the man had fallen.

About a hundred yards in, he saw the man struggling just ahead. Jones leveled the shotgun.

"Stop now!" he shouted.

The man turned, his automatic still in his hand.

"Drop the gun now, or I'll blow your head off," Jones yelled, moving forward. "If you hit me you'll freeze to death before finding shelter."

He pointed the light straight at the man's face to make it difficult for him to see. Holding his empty hand over his eyes, the man paused only a second before pitching his pistol into the snow.

"On the ground face down," the deputy ordered. Stepping to the man's side and bending down, he forced his arms behind and clicked on handcuffs. The man was bleeding from one hand but didn't appear wounded anywhere else. Before pulling his prisoner to his feet, Jones looked for the gun but didn't see it. He gave the man a pat-down and took his wallet before pushing him along, using the same tracks they made coming in. When he got back to the car, he could hear sirens from the backup. It had taken them about 15 minutes to arrive.

Jones locked the man in the back seat of his patrol car and started toward the rental truck in the ditch. He paused, opened the man's wallet and found his driver's license. "Now let's see, Miguel Martinez, what was worth your friend getting killed for," he said. He walked to the truck and opened the load doors. Inside were stacks and stacks of 50-pound barrels clearly marked ephedrine. "Holy shit," Jones said aloud. "The meth mother load. No wonder these guys were scared."

There were a half dozen patrol cars, one from the state police, three from the Canon City force, two more deputy's cars, plus the ambulance all around him. Flares were going. The chief deputy rolled up next and rushed over to Jones.

"For Christ's sake, Will, are you all right? Sit down over here."

Now the young officer felt his knees shake and was glad to be led to his own car, where he sat suddenly like his strings were cut. His chief yelled for the medics who were inspecting the body: "Forget the motherfucker on the ground, he's dead, our guy is wounded over here."

"Just a nick," Jones protested. "Send someone out to the arrest point. They'll find his handgun in the snow near where I put him on the ground."

"Great work," the chief deputy said. You've got a great future in law enforcement if you don't let this scare you away" He patted Jones' shoulder and moved aside as the medics arrived to bandage his ear. "Give him a tranquilizer too if you have one."

Turning back to his deputy, he gave him a bright smile, "Hey, deputy, Happy New Year. Don't you think so?" All considered, Jones sure did.

25

Insistent ringing jolted Tanner from the dreamy aftermath of his champagne romp. The digital clock showed 2 a.m. The television was still on and broadcasting a New Year's show from California. Sally softly grunted and pulled a pillow over her head. Tanner pulled the receiver to his mouth without raising his head, "Mumph."

He dimly recognized Moore's voice: "Sam. Things have busted wide open and you gotta rise and shine. This is your case and we need you here."

Tanner was awake now and sitting up. Sally started to raise up but he reached an arm over and gently pushed her down. "Not family," he reassured. "Business."

Moore launched into a quick description of the night's shooting and the discovery of two tons of ephedrine in a truck operated by Miguel Martinez and a flunky, who was shot and killed by a sheriff's deputy. He said the Fremont County officers had immediately notified DEA because of the chemical. "Where are you now?" Tanner asked

"I'm at the site, three and a half miles north of Canon City on State Road 9. You need to get to the Fremont County Jail as soon as you can. Have you been celebrating?"

"I was in bed by 11."

"Then you may be the only guy I can find who's sober.

"Groton know?"

"I'll leave that to you. How long before you can get here?"

"An hour or so, wide open."

Tanner hung up, grabbed a shirt and pants and a pair snow boots. He put in a call to Groton as he sat and slipped into his pants. The phone rang five times before Groton answered and Tanner launched into his explanation, not bothering to apologize for waking him.

"I'm on the way to Canon City, Josh. We're going to have to get an assistant U.S. attorney on the job in Denver and locate a magistrate. I think we'll need a bushel of warrants. I'll call you when I get to Fremont County."

"I'll head for the office. I'll get Tom Hayden and Charles Gadsen down there and call Assistant U. S. Attorney Patrick Toner in Denver and Hayden can go up there with the list of needs etc."

As he was pulling on his boots, Tanner said to Sally, "It's the beginning of the end of this business, babe. I'll see you when I see you, could be several days. I'll stuff a change of clothes in my duffle and I have a suit and tie at the office. I'll stay in touch but it won't be hourly."

He grabbed his night bag and clumped down the stairs. In the kitchen by a cabinet he opened a high panel were he kept his little hideaway .38 and stuffed it his ankle holster. He checked his Glock, grabbed a box of shotgun shells from the garage and opened the trunk of his company car and pulled out his bullet-proof vest and 12 -gauge. He didn't really think he'd need all the hardware because much of the next day would be spent on paperwork and pulling together teams for the searches and arrests. He slipped into the vest and threw a heavy sweater and a blue ATF jacket on the backseat. He was on his way fifteen minutes after Moore's call. Once out of his neighborhood he turned on the flashing lights and pushed the accelerator as fast as he thought the roads would handle, a skittery 65.

He was 20 minutes into the drive when his radio blared. Groton.

"Are you there?"

"No, I'm in Vegas."

"Okay, smart ass. I'll be in the office in five more minutes, keep me advised.

Five minutes later Groton rang back. "I've been thinking we treat all these cases separately though they're all connected. We take down the Martinez brothers and then Pacheco's troops and then Kennedy's car crew. We can leave Marsh and Crowe and their operation to the last. That means keeping you out of the spotlight and doing the dirty for a while. You up for that?"

"I am."

"Good." He hung up.

The sky had cleared to a riot of stars when Tanner drove into the Fremont Jail parking lot. He grabbed his coat from the back seat and headed down the walk to the entrance, flashed his credentials to the deputy on duty and was told to skip the metal detector.

"I've seen you before," the young deputy told him. 'Big case here, Agent Tanner. A guy from the DEA is ahead of you and waiting in the room off to the left. We're holding a prisoner in the preliminary lock up."

"Is there a coffee machine around here, deputy?" Tanner asked.

"Better than that. We just made a fresh pot inside the jail kitchen. I'll bring you some. Go ahead into the conference room."

Moore was sitting at the end of a conference table going over a file when Tanner entered. He looked up and grinned.

"We hit the Comstock, old buddy," he said exuberantly. "Martinez wants to give it all up in exchange for immunity or a light sentence. That means his brothers, all the vitamin plant guys who provided the ephedrine, the cookers, delivery people, the whole frigging business. He's scared shitless he's going to be charged with attempted murder of a police officer. He's offering up locations of their stash in both Fremont and Park Counties."

There was a knock on the door and a trustee came into the room with a pot of coffee, cups and cream and sugar. The agents thanked him and waited until he was out the door before continuing their conversation.

"Well, hell, we'll just call out the troops," Tanner said. "I can take care of that." He called the U.S. attorney's office in Denver to explain Martinez demands.

The Assistant U.S. Attorney in Denver asked several questions about the legitimacy of the information and whether all procedures had been followed. He was fascinated by Moore's description of the shoot out and arrest of Martinez.

"I don't like making deals ahead of time," he said. "But you can tell him that if what he gives us is as productive as we have been led to believe, I will recommend to the judge that his sentence be no more than 10 years for his cooperation in ending this."

Sherry Sanford parked her Viper in the underground garage of Marsh's apartment building about 10 that night. She wore a red silk dress she knew would rev his engine and carried an overnight bag. She had hopes, but some unease nagged at her. It wasn't like him to suddenly warm up after they'd fought, and she'd been pretty sure his interest in her was fading

She shook off the feeling and walked the few feet to the elevator to take her directly to his top floor apartment—what he liked to brag about was his Penthouse, with its expanse of glass looking out at the mountains. His apartment, Sherry often thought, was Marsh's best feature. The living room had a cathedral ceiling, a large fireplace and enough electronic gizmos to stock a Best Buy. Before the housing crash Marsh had boasted it was worth more than a million.

He was smiling as he opened the door, took her coat and gave an appreciative whistle for her clingy dress. He nodded toward the bar in the corner and said, "I think we'll stay in tonight, if you don't mind. Crowe is coming over later and I have another friend here."

Sherry looked up to see blonde woman come out of the master bedroom. A man would have taken in the long legs and high breasts. Sherry saw dark roots and dead eyes. This she knew instantly was the other girl and started to turn and leave but realized her keys and ID and money were in her coat that Jay Ray had taken. Should she make an excuse and try to leave? Looking at Marsh she knew he already had been into the meth, and a sudden move by her to get out would trigger his temper

As she was deciding he said, "Easy, baby," taking her arm firmly and steering her toward the couch. "Anna's here for Ray. Brenda got some sort of bug and begged off for the evening. I thought she was going to call you. C'mon, have a drink and relax." It came more as an order than suggestion. He turned to the blonde and said, "Anna, you mind getting the munchies out of the fridge?" He watched her go into the kitchen, and said to Sherry in a low voice, "She's yesterday, and gone tomorrow. I've been missing you."

Sherry wasn't sure she believed him, but decided to make the best of the situation. "Okay you sonofabitch, but don't try to get me into one of your threesomes. I'm in no mood and she ain't my type." She went to the bar, filled a glass with ice and poured an inch of vodka. "Let's party."

Marsh opened a vile of white powder, poured it out and used his flick-blade to draw three lines on the surface of the bar. She sniffed half a line into one nostril and the rest of it in the other. She dabbed at her nose and sipped the vodka. Things were looking better, she thought. Marsh called for Anna who came back in with a tray of cheeses and pate and crackers. Anna did the second line of coke and Marsh the third. The lights were low and the music soft.

26

The next twelve hours went by in a blur for Tanner. A forty-person task force was formed to target new locations supplied by Martinez, as well as those earlier pinpointed by Tanner and Moore, for a roundup that fanned across five counties seeking Maria and Ramon Pacheco and both the remaining Martinez brothers, Ernesto and Emilio.

Tanner kept a low profile for the time being to preserve his cover, personally arresting only Kennedy, who began crying. Tanner assured him his continued cooperation would likely get him only a nickel sentence, but, "If you don't quit the blubbering, I'll convince 'em to tack another five onto it." He passed him a cell phone and told him to call every one of his car boosters and to come to a meeting in the next hour. Kennedy reached three, who were arrested as they arrived, and warrants were issued for three others.

Moore and Gadsen led the team that burst into Maria Pacheco's modest bungalow and discovered a cache of ledgers going back fifteen years. Maria was a meticulous if misguided bookkeeper, listing dates and amounts of drugs distributed and even gun sales, linking suppliers to buyers and providing prosecutors in days ahead with an encyclopedia of her crimes.

"She didn't seem especially upset that it was over," Moore told Tanner afterward. "She acted almost relieved, like she'd expected something worse than us to be coming through her door."

A team snagged Ramon Pacheco as he walked slowly up the steps to his house, phone at his ear. Ramon hadn't been able to reach anybody and was greatly pissed about it. He didn't understand why the feds were rousting him now and tried to explain that the recent warrant that had turned up drugs and guns in his house was not good because some dumbass agent had forgotten to sign it. It was explained to him to shut up and spread 'em.

Tanner led another team to a property given up by Martinez, where they found a ramshackle house trailer and a pole barn. An officer poking into the barn caught his trousers on a wire that stuck about six inches out of the wall, gave it a tug and a panel collapsed outward exposing three AK47s. They began pulling down wallboard all round the shed and found AKs behind every one, a total of twenty-two fully automatic weapons.

In the trailer Tanner was flabbergasted to find a briefcase full of $100 bills lying on a bunk. When counted, the money came to $300,000. Underneath sleeping bags on the floor of the trailer he discovered forty more pistols and revolvers.

So it went. By 5 p.m. there had been sixty arrests and weaponry found at fourteen different locations, a downtown garage with eleven stolen cars, an estimated hundred pounds of processed crystal meth, two more satchels of cash as yet uncounted and half a dozen barrels of ephedrine buried at several mountain properties with more being uncovered.

Tanner got home at 8:15 and fell asleep on the couch while Sally was heating his dinner. She pulled off his boots, covered him with a down throw and turned off the lights, muttering, "Some New Years."

Sometime after midnight Tanner had to get up and relieve the pressure from the coffee that had kept him on his feet for most of the previous twenty-four hours. He was standing over the bowl thinking he'd never get done and back to the couch when he felt his cell phone vibrating in his pocket. He looked and saw it was Marsh.

"Jay Ray!" he exclaimed, adding truthfully, "I've been trying to get hold of you."

Marsh was raving. "Are you watching the tube? It's all over the news, biggest drug and guns bust in Colorado ever. My whole network's being rolled up. I can't get anybody to answer."

"No," Tanner said, "I'm in Durango, haven't had time for TV, don't know a thing about it."

"It's the feds. They came down like an avalanche on the Martinez's and Pachecos. It's a disaster. I can't get anybody to answer. I need to see you, man."

Tanner explained he was snowed in for the night but he'd get on the road in the morning as soon as he heard that Wolf Creek Pass was clear.

"Well shit," said Marsh. "I need you now."

Tanner let that hang and then said, "I'm a free agent, remember that. I understand you got troubles, but I haven't decided they're my problem. You'll see me when I get there."

As he clicked off Tanner thought he heard a woman crying in the background.

The paperwork and interviewing of prisoners and working out who had competing jurisdictions would take months to get through. While this was a federal case overall, state and locals also had charges to file. Every agent who'd been in on the case from the beginning hated this end of it, including the fact they would be tied up for weeks or months testifying in trials when it came to that. They hoped many would plead out for leniency. That, of course, would not be true of all the principals. Maria Pacheco really had nobody to rat out, her seized bookkeeping doing that for her. Ramon Pacheco had no wriggle room. He was toast on tape. One Martinez was singing for the feds, another had clammed and the third was in the wind. Marsh and Crowe, too, had eluded the roundup. Tanner's job was to lure them on and bring them in.

But he knew, listening to Marsh on the phone, to meet him on his own ground before everything was in place was a mistake he wouldn't make.

27

Early on the morning of the second day of the New Year, Tom Wingate, a tired driver for the Kaytie Cookie Company, was just breaking his big blue van just outside of Limon, Colorado. He'd stopped a few miles back for breakfast and now the coffee he'd drunk was having it's effect. He pulled to the shoulder just south of a rutted hunting track road and stood with his back against his truck. He stood there gazing out on dreary flats covered with a light snow and caught a flash of red maybe thirty yards away. He shrugged, zipped his pants and started for the cab but out of the corner of his eye caught more of the red. He snugged the zipper of his heavy jacket and walked into the unfenced field.

When he was a few yards away, stopped as he realized what he was seeing. The red was torn fabric and he realized a horror in front of him. A woman's body stretched out on the ground and a trail of brown that had to be dried blood stained the ground where she'd either crawled or been dragged. Her face and hands had been smeared with what looked to him like feces.

Wingate turned and ran to the truck, pulled out his cell phone and dialed 911. When the operator answered his voice shook and it was hard for him to explain what he had seen. The slowest half hour of Wingate's life passed before a highway patrol car pulled up and Wingate climbed out of the truck to point. The trooper moved out into the field, spent a few minutes there and hurried back to call for backup. It was noon when the coroner approved removal of the body. He had studied violent death for thirty years and there few things humans did to each other that he couldn't cleanse from his mind. This was one that stuck there. The young woman had been shot several times, her arms taking most of the bullets as she tried to ward them off. She had been beaten, and stabbed, and was still alive when left out in that field. There were ample signs she had crawled some fifty yards toward the highway before dying just short of it. Whoever did this had smeared her with peanut butter, apparently intending that predators would be attracted and eat her remains. It hadn't happened. The real animal was the one who'd left her like that.

Tanner was up to his ass in government form that afternoon when Moore stuck his head in the door. "I just got a call from CSPD about a murder out by Limon. Fingerprints belong to a Sherry Sanford. Marsh's squeeze, right?"

Tanner winced. "They certain?"

"Very. State ran the prints through national ID system and discovered she was there on priors for prostitution

"Was she badly abused?"

"According to the locals, she was beaten, shot, stabbed, possibly strangled some for fun and, can you believe it, smeared with peanut butter. They speculate the bastard who did it wanted her eaten by the vermin."

Tanner was shaken. If he'd gone there when called, maybe he could have stopped it. He clumped down to Groton's office and reported Sanford's death.

"I have an idea," he said.

28

Tanner's plan was simple. He'd meet Marsh in a public place and pay with marked cash for the promised C-4 and the automatic rifles. With the buy recorded, backup would converge and shut down the last big cog in the wrecked meth machine. He called at noon, "Meet me at the Golden Corral in Manitou."

Marsh had been demanding Tanner's help but now was wary, "Why there?"

"I'm out that way. Nobody pays any attention to you there. Come about 3:15 when the lunch crowd is finished."

Tanner was sitting at a table for four in a corner sipping coffee when Marsh walked in, looking nervously around the empty restaurant before making his way to the back. Pulling out his chair he said, "It's all gone to shit. I can't believe it fell apart so quick." Tanner said nothing and Marsh continued. "I've been trying to get to you for two days. Really could have used you," he said, petulant. "What can you do now?"

Tanner shrugged and spread his hands. "Only thing I can do. I'm getting the hell out of here before somebody names to me. But I need that last package to meet obligations before I relocate. The plastic stuff, and the AKs you said you had. I've got the cash. Let's do it now."

Marsh gave a sour smile. "I'm outa here, too. I stick around and it's damn sure somebody behind bars is gonna give me up. So yeah, we help each other. Can you cover a couple pounds of meth, too? Also I'm looking to unload a Dodge Viper with less than 20,000 miles on it."

"Really. When did you get that?"

"An old girlfriend had to go away. Signed it over for some favors owed. It's yours for walking around money. How's ten grand? It's worth sixty. And ten for the meth?"

"Sounds okay.

"Let's get gone."

They agreed to meet again at six, at a parking lot off I-25 just inside the Manitou exit. Tanner said he would be bringing his friend George to help with the transfer. Marsh agreed: "Crowe'll be with me for the same reason. He'll drive his car and I'll drive the Viper and leave it with you. I'll have the stuff in the trunk."

Tanner nosed his pickup against a retaining wall protecting the lot from the highway. Winkler in the passenger seat keyed his mic, and Gadsen and Hayden in a panel truck twenty feet away clicked back they were receiving. It was 45 minutes ahead of schedule.

At five to six, a black Viper followed by a Toyota 4-Runner pulled into the lot and headed for the pickup, backing into spaces next to the truck. Tanner and Winkler were sitting now in the bed of the truck with the gate down, dangling their feet. They hopped down and shook hands with the two dealers and Tanner walked to the Viper, lookin it over closely and letting out a low whistle. "Some ride, all right," he said. Winkler nodded agreement, "What mileage you get?"

"Who gives a fuck in a Viper?" Marsh shot back and they all laughed.

"Fuck in a Viper, you have to be a contortionist," Winkler quipped and they laughed some more.

Marsh tossed the keys to Tanner who opened the trunk and pulled a blanket off a plastic square of meth and a package holding a waxy green block. He sniffed both, tested the meth and smiled. "The guns?"

"In the Toyota," said Marsh. He was jittery, eyes looking around the lot, resting on the panel truck a long beat, then back to Tanner. "No room for that many long guns in the Viper. They'll have to go in your pickup."

Tanner went to the SUV and inspected the stack of AKs, then to his pickup, opened the cab door and took out a briefcase. He handed it to Marsh.

"Fifty large. Open it and count it," he said.

Marsh normally would hand the case to Crowe and wait for

confirmation. Events of the last few days made him rush it. He opened the case thumbed through the bills and closed it.

"Okay. Nice going. Good deal and goodbye."

Both Crowe and Marsh had their backs to the parking lot and didn't notice the four agents in their blue jackets with the bright yellow ATF on the back coming up behind them, spread out and weapons drawn.

"Federal agents," Gadsen yelled. "Down on the ground, now, face down."

Tanner and Winkler both dropped and rolled toward the pickup.

Marsh paused but seeing firepower raised his hands and kneeled, slow and reluctant.

Tanner watched in horror as Crowe instinctively went for an automatic tucked in the waistband of his pants under his jacket. He fumbled it long enough for Tanner to raise up and hurl himself into Crowe, scrabbling for the gun.

"Goddamn it, Roy!" he shouted. "You'll get us killed."

His hand clamped Crowe's just as the automatic was clearing his pants and they strained, then came a deafening report, and Tanner felt Crowe's body stiffen and collapse. The dealer slipped down to the ground pulling Tanner with him.

"I'm fucked," Crowe said through gritted teeth. He had both hands pressed to his groin.

There was a surprising amount blood, bright arterial red, on Crowe's pants, pooling on the ground, covering Tanner's own left leg. He looked to where Marsh had stood. He was face down on the ground, too, now, his arms pulled behind his back and being cuffed, an agent kneeling on the small of his back.

"Oh shit, hurts," Crowe said, his face deathly white and eyes losing focus. He used what strength he had to mumble as Tanner leaned close, "Marsh killed Sherry. Bastard did terrible things to her, killed her. I couldn't stop him. Viper is hers. I'm sorry. Check his apartment."

The wire Tanner wore picked up his last words. Crowe convulsed and was still. Tanner himself felt suddenly faint himself. That had never happened and he was starting to feel embarrassed. He started to get up and couldn't. His thigh hurt like hell. What was wrong there? He suddenly sat and stared at it, stupidly.

"You okay, Sam?" Winkler asked.

Tanner didn't understand the question. "Uh," he said.

"Oh fuck," Winkler said. "Sam, bullet got you, too. Hey guys. . ."

It was the last Tanner heard. He was so tired. He needed to lie down. He rolled.

29

Jay Ray Marsh sat in the interview room of the El Paso County Jail, shackled to a steel ring on the floor. A deputy led a handcuffed George Winkler into the room, sat him opposite Marsh and bent to snap leg restraints to another ring on the floor, uncuffed him and left the room.

Marsh looked around and leaned forward, "Jesus, George, that went bad fast. Somebody gave us up and I'd love to know who. I thought it was this old girlfriend ratting me, but she was out of the picture before we set up the meet."

A minute dragged.

"It was Jack."

"Jack?"

"Yeah."

"Jack from Kansas?"

"Afraid so."

"How do you know that?"

Winkler reached in his orange jumpsuit's pocket and pulled a tape recorder and punched play. Out came Crowe's voice, "Marsh killed Sherry. Bastard did terrible things to her . . ."

Winkler punched stop.

"What the fuck?" Marsh leaned forward. "Where'd that come from?"

"Jack was wearing a wire."

"Fuck me. How'd you get it? How come they let you have that?"

Winkler reached in his pocket again and took out keys, bent down and unlocked the leg restraints, and stood.

"'Cause I'm CSP. And Jack is Sam Tanner of ATF. And you are, as you say, fucked. I couldn't resist fucking with you some more."

Winkler paused to let that soak in. Marsh sat stunned.

"They'll be in here soon as I walk out, to charge you with murder. We found Sherry's body. As you heard, we've got Crowe's dying words on the tape making you for the killing. A search of your penthouse turned up a slipper that's the match of one she had on her foot when found. We're running DNA tests on the bloodstains we found there. Wanna bet how that turns out?"

Marsh was shaking his head, slow.

"Oh yes. And Jack, excuse me, Sam Tanner of ATF, was seriously wounded during your arrest. So you'll face charges on that too. With what depends on his recovery."

Winkler walked to the door and paused, looking back. "By the way, you might like to know that the guy who found Sherry was a truck driver for Kaytie Cookies, where you were the big cheese before becoming a dipshit druggie. He used to work for you. Ain't that something? Kinda jogs your funny bone, don't it?"

Tanner woke thirsty. His throat was raw. His leg hurt like fire. The room was too bright and he was chilled. He grunted.

"That's what you have to say for yourself?" It was Sally's voice.

He looked where it came from, and she stood and came to the bed and softly squeezed his hand.

"What were you thinking?" she demanded. "We had a deal. A simple arrangement, I do the cooking and you don't get shot. Remember that?"

Sam swallowed. "Water," he said.

She poured a glass and held a straw to his lips. He drank and he smiled.

"You okay?" he asked.

"Why wouldn't I be? I didn't try to be faster than a speeding bullet."

Sam didn't hear it. He slept again.

Spring was over by the time the justice system had disposed of most of the cases.

Maria and Ramon Pacheco pleaded guilty and got 15-year sentences for cooperating.

Miguel Martinez got the 10 years he was promised for his help. But his brother Ernesto was given the maximum, life. It's what you get for keeping your mouth shut, is how it was explained to him. He said nothing to that, too. Efforts to find Emilio the hit man went nowhere, which summed up the village in Guatemala where he was hiding.

JoJo Kennedy got five years and the expectation of being out in two and a half. His drivers, who couldn't give him up since he'd already sung, went on 10 to 20 raps for interstate transportation of stolen cars.

Marsh pleaded out. The tape, the slipper, the blood and Tanner's pending testimony convinced him to take a deal rather than risk death penalty in state court. The man who bragged about never being arrested got life, plus forty and no possibility of parole.

Anna, Marsh's replacement girlfriend, was given immunity from prosecution for telling agents that she had been there when Marsh tortured Sherry Sanford. She was there when he put Sheri in the car, she said. He had threatened her life if she called the police, she claimed, and Marsh was in no position to dispute that. She walked

Josh Groton went to a headquarters job in Washington. He moved up a grade, took up trap shooting on weekends, and when his old dachshund Bismarck died his wife got a tiny gray poodle. It yapped. Groton insisted on naming it Skeet.

When he was released from the hospital, Tanner flew to Washington for a commendation. He had another promising case going in Colorado Springs that seemed destined to be more bizarre than the last one. With Groton gone and Gadsen on the way to a headquarters desk job, the prospect of a new boss and street partner wasn't comforting. But he shrugged it off a just part of the game he loved.

Tanner never wanted to leave here. He knew, though, his wife and the suits in Washington had it right, it soon would be time to get off the street. He understood, too, he was at that crossroad he came to now and again, where he looked this way and that way and asked himself, what was the point of risking his life for government salary in a cause the government didn't believe in? There were at last count 308 million people and just about the same number of guns, one for everyone in the land of the free, home of the bang. In his lifetime he could expect to see it reach 400 million Americans and, just as sure, 400 million guns in their hands. And his agency hardly had one friend in Congress.

He stood and slipped into his jacket. He took the elevator down and walked outside where the greening slopes were shining in the June sun, and he looked up at them. He could feel the warm dry breeze on his face. He made a smile and it was wistful. Never mind what came of it, out there in the wind was the right place to be.

Dan Thomasson is a veteran newspaper correspondent and news executive who resides in the District of Columbia and currently writes two nationally syndicated columns a week

Jack Lang is a writer living on the Eastern Shore of Maryland.